LONGARM DREW HIS GUN AND FIRED...

The report of his gun rattled along the street. The bullet struck the boar between the eyes, and the animal staggered slightly and then toppled on its side at the washgirl's bare feet.

Unable to speak, the Mexican girl stood unmoving, her face frozen in terror.

"Are you all right?" Longarm asked.

The girl started, as if awakened from a dream. "*Sí, Señor.*" Her great olive-black eyes were fixed on his face, and she nodded, but did not take her gaze from him...

Also in the LONGARM series from Jove

TABOR EVANS

LONGARM

IN SILVER CITY

A JOVE BOOK

LONGARM IN SILVER CITY

A Jove Book / published by arrangement with
the author

PRINTING HISTORY
Jove edition / January 1982
Second printing / August 1982
Third printing / April 1983

ISBN: 0-515-07413-6

Jove books are published by Jove Publications, Inc.,
200 Madison Avenue, New York, N.Y. 10016. The words
"A JOVE BOOK" and the "J" with sunburst are trademarks
belonging to Jove Publications, Inc.

PRINTED IN THE UNITED STATES OF AMERICA

Chapter 1

Longarm sniffed trouble like a steer catching the scent of water in the middle of alkali flats.

What's eatin' at me? he inquired savagely, behind that polite mask of his face where no one could hear and become unduly alarmed at some hatchet-faced jasper talking to himself.

All he knew was that some unwanted embroilment lurked just up the trail. He knew this, even when he had nothing to go on except instinct. And he wasn't about to start mistrusting his instincts; they'd kept him alive down a lot of backtrails.

He scowled at the backs of his callused hands. What the contention might be and how far along the trace, he couldn't be sure, but like that thirsty steer sniffing the air, he prickled with the dead-certain feeling that it was there, waiting.

His first inkling of wrong struck him when his through-coach going south stopped at Socorro in the blaze of a hot, dry morning. Nothing unusual in a scheduled stop, but the driver poked his bewhiskered face in the tonneau window and made it all as odd as hell.

1

"You're gettin' off here, Mr. Long." The driver's hoarse voice was a bellow, even when pitched in a friendly and conversational tone.

Something stirred deep inside Longarm's belly, that faint fluttering of alarm. "Why?"

The driver grinned at him, withdrew, and swung up on the iron rungs. Longarm saw his new hard-leather, government-issue bag untied from the baggage-stacked roofing and thrown casually into the gray dirt outside the adobe way station.

"What the hell," Longarm protested. "I might have liquor in there."

The bearded driver just smiled at him and shrugged. "Hope so, Mr. Long. You'll plumb need it where you're goin'."

The driver turned away as Longarm stepped down from the battered old stagecoach. He caught the big man's arm lightly, but detained him firmly. "How come you're puttin' me off here? I got a through ticket."

"Yep." The man nodded his head. "All the way to Silver City."

"Do I have to tell you this is Socorro?"

"Reckoned it to be." The driver nodded his head again and spat a brown glob of tobacco juice into the dirt between them. "You're goin' on to Silver City. But we ain't headed that way, mister. We follow the Old Spanish Trail 'longside the Rio Grandy, south to Las Cruces." He bobbed his battered Stetson toward a gleaming coach parked carefully in the shade of a cottonwood. "That there is your coach. You'll travel to hell in style, anyhow. Come to think of it, that there coach do resemble a hearse, now don't it?"

He slapped his fat leg and walked away laughing.

Carrying his dust-smeared bag, Longarm limped over to the stylish coach. His gimpy walk resulted from no bodily injury except the total exhaustion of an eternal stagecoach ride southwest from Denver, plus the cramped position of his long legs in the narrow space between facing seats designed for midgets. Also, an ill-healed bullet wound nagged at the fringes of his consciousness. One thing about a gun wound: it plain hurt, going in and coming out. And even when it cured up and scarred over, it twinged irregularly, just to remind you.

2

The driver was right, this carriage did look like one of those stylish hearses used in Denver when some political bigwig, silver mine operator, or first-family member kicked off.

He exhaled, surveying the carriage. It boasted narrow steel-rimmed wheels. Leaf-spring thoroughbraces were slung to absorb some of the roadshock. No doubt, this vehicle was the finest example of luxury-equipage craft. Its interior was upholstered in dark blue velvet; facing seats, with ample knee room, were deeply padded and plush. Framed glass windows slid up and down on cord straps in the door, for comfort in any kind of weather.

The graceful body, of finest hand-rubbed mahogany, shone until he could glimpse his travel-weary reflection in its burnished depths. It was like looking at himself in a dark mirror.

Longarm was none too elated or reassured by what he saw. His gray flannel shirt bore long, heavy sweat streaks. In the close, breathless heat of that stagecoach across the barren white New Mexico desert, he was beginning to smell old and used.

He admitted he still looked lean and hard enough to cut the mustard—muscular, with shoulders that strained the fabric of his frock coat. Time, pitiless suns, and burning snows had wind-cured his rawboned face to a saddle-leather brown. No softness was exposed in the gunmetal blue of his sun-faded eyes, either. They remained young, watchful, and wary. He watched his reflection touch at its neatly waxed longhorn mustache, proud and flaring between a sharp-hewn nose and a taut-lipped mouth. His snuff-brown Stetson, its crown telescoped in the Colorado fashion, low over his dark brows, positioned carefully, slightly forward, cavalry-style, to shade and almost conceal his eyes.

He sighed and turned away. When a man began to go to fat in his business, it was time to rack the guns. Trouble moved fast, and you had to be ready—to run it down or, if need be, to outrun it for a second chance another day.

He smiled grimly, chewing at his unlit two-for-a-nickel cheroot. Ever since he'd run away from his home in West-by God-Virginia to ride in the big war, he'd been dealing with trouble, one way or another.

He shook his head, sweating in the dead heat and silence

3

of the little trail town. In all those years, he'd never become too damned enamored of trouble, either. He could take it or leave it.

"Por favor! Por favor! Cuidado, Señor!"

Three hostlers, half-running, led a team of harnessed horses around the adobe building and hitched them to the coach. Longarm sagged in the shade of the dust-hung, leaf-sagging cottonwood, waiting.

The stablehands argued dispassionately but intensely in broken English about some disagreement from the previous night over a town girl named Lupe. They did not glance again toward Longarm.

When the horses were hitched in place and the lines carefully wrapped and waiting around the whipstock on the carriage boot, the three men plodded back around the building in the blazing sun, still arguing desultorily.

"Howdy, friend. You the fare going to Silver City on this coach with us?"

Longarm turned, nodding. This medium-tall man was impressive looking, and one recognized him on sight as *un hombre rico,* a man of untold affluence, power, position, and unquestioned authority, all of which he wore as easily as he sported the tailored suit of finest brown worsted, impeccable matching Stetson flat-crown, and hand-tooled, Mexican-ornamented brown boots with silver tips. His hands were pinkly scrubbed, the nails recently manicured and buffed. But he didn't look like a fop or a dandy. He looked like a man who had earned every dollar of his considerable wealth one at a time, with no help from anybody. Those hands had once borne scars and calluses, even if time had healed and softened them, and those smiling blue eyes carried dark secrets in their depths.

This was a world-smart man, outgoing, free-handed, and congenial, with the bluff, hearty openness of the Westerner; but he was wary and on guard at the same time.

"This crate is mine," the man said. He drew his palm along its polished beauty, then thrust out his hand. Longarm shook it, finding the grip strong and unrelenting. "What I do is, I let the stage people use it for public conveyance whenever I travel out of Silver City. Hate fiercely to ride anywhere alone, you know. I figure man's naturally a socializing animal. By the

4

way, the name's W. W. Meriman. Might be you've heard of me."

Longarm smiled and nodded at the modest suggestion. He knew W. W. Meriman, all right. The name Meriman was big even in Denver, the center of the silver market. Among other things, Meriman owned silver mines, smelters, and land all through Grant County. "I've heard," he said.

Meriman grinned. "What's your handle, friend?"

"Custis Long."

Meriman peered up at him, still grinning. "You're a big 'un, ain't you? Six-two? Six-three? Something like that?"

"Something like that. Being a whole foot longer than the average male ain't all that great. Beds ain't long enough. Some doors ain't tall enough. And you can't even hide in crowds."

"Do a lot of hiding, do you?"

Longarm grinned. "If you're asking what my trade is, I'm a lawman."

"Son of a gun. Might have suspected as much. I reckon when you speak, people listen, huh?"

"That's one of the things I've heard about *you.*"

Meriman laughed. "That's my money people listen to. You got enough money, folks bow and scrape to you no matter what kind of turd you might be personally."

Longarm shrugged. "A man has enough money, he can afford to be a turd."

"I reckon." Meriman shook his head, considering it all. "But you know, I never set out to pile up a lot of money in banks. For what? For somebody to fight over when I'm dead? Hell, making money was a sideline for me. A kind of fringe benefit. When I massed up too much, I'd run out and try to spend it off—on the usual trinkets, straight whiskey, crooked cards, and laughing women. Always have loved myself a laughing woman. But it seemed like I couldn't spend it fast enough, and it kept sticking in my accounts, or coming back double every dime I spent. You fool around with mining long enough—in the right place and at the right time—and that's liable to happen.

"Hell, I contracted the prospecting fever when I was a pecker-sized kid. I left home with a few greenbacks that nobody wanted to take in them days—hell, I never could get a Mexican to accept paper money. *Nada. Nada.* They wanted gold or silver.

"Anyhow, I pitched in with some footloose hombres who owned a mule team. I was hired to punch along the lead mule. That's all right until you try to ford a stream. You ever forded a creek with a donkey or a mule?"

"A few times."

"Mighty peculiar thing I learned from that mule. No matter how deep or swift a creek was, them danged animals always stopped to crap right in the middle of it, and all hell couldn't move them until they dumped their load and got ready to move on. By then, bedding was usually soaked through, and any flour would be wet and useless.

"Anyhow, first pay strike I ever made was in Elizabeth Town. It was on Ute Creek and panned out pretty good. Placer mining was new to me, but it wasn't long before I knew how to detect the color in a pan. We panned old river beds and sifted through diggings. Came on some bedrock and hit some mean pay streaks. First deposits I ever worked were shallow, and I got them out with a pick and shovel. Saw a lot of hydraulic-pressure mining, but that looked like too much work for a young kid.

"I liked working with them sluice boxes. Some of them were three or four hundred feet long. We set up a fair outfit— long-tom, sluice box, and flume. The long-tom looked like a coffin set up on a trestle and tipped toward the sluice box.

"Those old sluice boxes we used to build of raw, rough lumber, like a trough with both ends open. Slats or riffles were laid crosswise in the bottom of the sluice. The riffles caught the free metal. We learned all the tricks. Used mercury to help catch the gold, 'cause gold is drawn to quicksilver, you know. When quicksilver was used, you ended up with a mess of metal, so you had to clean up once a week or so.

"We learned to separate the gold from quicksilver or any other foreign metals. This was called cupelling. The metal was put in a porous bone-ash cup, set in a furnace, and exposed to a blast of air. Oxidized metal dropped into the pores of the cup, whilst the mercury was vaporized and caught in the chimney and used again. Only pure gold was left in the cupel.

"I soon got so I could tell a rich pay streak from a poor

one. I took to mining like a pig takes to warm mud. But I got itchy feet, and before long I sold out my half to a good claim and headed south with a horse and pack mule. I traveled light— a few groceries, Arbuckle coffee, slab of salt bacon, and a sack of flour that I soon learned to carry on my head when we crossed creeks.

"Well, hell, I ended up down in the Sierra Diablo mountain ranges. That's what we called it, them days. Devil Mountains. Folks call it the Black Range now.

"I was young and full of vinegar and thought I knew all there was to know about mining—and I did know placer mining pretty fair—but down in the Black Range country, you didn't get much gold and damned little silver that easy. You blasted it out of hard rock down here, or you didn't get it at all."

A tall, rail-thin man in Levi's, scuffed boots, and a denim jacket sauntered out of the adobe hut and crossed the sun-baked yard toward the shade of the cottonwood. He picked at his teeth with a whittled pine stick and sucked air through his cavities. He bowed his head and spoke with a lot of respect. "We ought to be headin' out soon, Mr. Meriman. Them other folks have et and all."

"Ready any time you are, Tom-Tom," Meriman said. He nodded toward Longarm. "This here is lawman Custis Long. Tom-Tom's one hell of a driver, Mr. Long. Been with me 'most twelve years now—and 'cept for almost gettin' our scalps lifted by Victorio's Chiricahua Apaches a few times, he's done right well."

Tom-Tom bobbed his head toward Longarm. "You a U. S. marshal, huh?"

Longarm winced slightly. Nobody had said who he worked for. That nagging sense of uneasiness buzzed around him again, as pesky as a deerfly.

He said nothing. Tom-Tom placed his bag on the roof baggage rack, then stacked W. W. Meriman's three calf-leather bags atop it. Tom-Tom was still hanging on the side rungs when a big voice, used to making itself heard in range gales, called from the door of the stage stop: "Stay up there, Tom-Tom. Got a couple valises for you."

Two small Mexican boys ran with the suitcases and handed them up to Tom-Tom, squinting against the sun. The aging man tossed each of them a silver coin and the boys backed away, grinning.

"Doesn't take much to make a Mexican kid happy, does it?" he said. Then his eyes widened. "Well, damn my soul! Longarm! Why, I haven't seen you since you visited us in Lincoln County that time. Nobody killed you off yet, huh?"

"Not yet, Mr. Chisum."

John Chisum wrung Longarm's hand. He said, "What in hell are you doing down this way?"

Something in Chisum's tone convinced Longarm that his business in Silver City, were he to explain it to the millionaire rancher, would be less than a surprise. So far, three out of three had known he was in the area, and very likely they knew why.

"They send me around to stir up trouble when there ain't any, Mr. Chisum," Longarm said.

Something flickered across Chisum's eyes, but he smiled and the big voice boomed. "You've already made the acquaintance of W. W. Meriman, huh? Did he tell you about his trip to New York City yet?"

"Not yet."

Meriman smiled and Chisum laughed aloud. "You're going to think I'm lying, Longarm. You've got to know W. W. Meriman like I do to believe it. He has the reputation for plain demolishing whole saloons when he gets likkered up enough. Word come back that he destroyed several saloons right on Broadway. He made a speech on the corner of Forty-second and Broadway, in front of one of the saloons he personally put out of business temporarily. You know what he told those good people of New York? He told them that they lived too far from Silver City ever to amount to anything!"

W. W. Meriman smiled in a modest way. "It seemed no more than a reasonable statement of fact to me," he said.

John Chisum climbed into the coach and sat down, breathing heavily. Age was an enemy the old cattleman couldn't conquer.

Longarm watched Chisum settle in the far corner of the tonneau, facing forward. It was as if this were the best seat, reserved for the Lincoln County stockman.

Watching the rancher, Longarm decided that Chisum hadn't changed much. He was a spare man, his skin the color and

8

texture of old, chewed leather. He wore boots as scuffed and broken as Tom-Tom's, with the bottoms of his frayed and faded Levi's tucked inside. His long, gaunt face narrowed to a jutting jaw. His hawk nose reared prominently, his graying brows were thick, his salt-and-pepper mustache full and bushy. The dark, piercing eyes regarded Longarm with something like suspicion.

"You'll have to get down to my place for a visit again soon, Marshal," he said.

"I sure will if I have time, sir."

"Nobody will try to shoot you this time," Chisum said, laughing.

Longarm was saved from answering by the arrival of the next passenger.

This gentleman was distinguished looking, with a pink, steak-fed face, and pale eyes under thick brows. In his early forties, he was not in the same financial class with Meriman or Chisum. His black suit and store-bought, high-topped black shoes were reasonably priced and advertised that the man lived on a government salary, and Longarm knew this wasn't easy.

"Morning, Judge McLoomis," W. W. Meriman said. His voice was hearty, though his blue eyes didn't manage to smile. "Good to have you along."

"Always a rare pleasure to be in your company, sir," Judge McLoomis said. He nodded his head, smiling, and removed his derby hat. His high forehead rose to prematurely gray hair, brushed back in waves, collar-length. "You're always the life of any gathering, W. W."

"A born politician," Meriman said to Longarm. "You'll seldom hear Judge Lynch McLoomis say a wrong thing, or an unpolitic thing, or an unpopular thing. Sometimes what he says don't make sense, but—"

"Maybe it just doesn't make sense to those who don't want to understand, W. W.," Judge McLoomis said with a mildly wry smile. He glanced at Longarm and extended his hand, with something like a look of relief flooding his florid face. "You're the federal marshal, eh? I wondered how long it would be before they sent one of you fellows down here."

Longarm shook the judge's hand, but he was not about to play stupid for them. He said, "Good to meet you, Judge. But

9

I still don't understand. I came on the quiet, ahead of time. What I'd like to know is, how'd every one of you people—including Tom-Tom the driver—know who I am, and what I'm doing here?"

Judge Lynch McLoomis's pink face flushed. He glanced around, confused. Inside the coach, John Chisum laughed. "Looks like Judge Lynch McLoomis is human after all, doesn't it? He can put his foot in his mouth just like any of us ordinary folks."

Judge McLoomis sighed and faced Longarm. He tried to smile, without a great deal of success. "We've all just come back from the territorial legislative session in Santa Fe, Mr. Long. All the talk up there was about the trouble festering and ready to burst in Silver City, and what the federal government was going to do about it when we couldn't get action from the army, the legislature, or Governor Wallace."

"I hope you fellows aren't barking up the wrong tree," Longarm said. "I'm here on a plain, simple mission."

"They all are," Chisum said. "I warn you, boy. Nothing is as simple as it seems in Silver City these days."

"Except maybe some of the people," Judge McLoomis said. "Everybody wants to talk, and nobody wants to listen. As I've said a dozen times, there are federal laws, and once you break them, you can count on Uncle Sam sending somebody in."

Nobody bothered to answer Judge McLoomis. Neither Chisum nor Meriman seemed overly impressed by the magistrate, though that in itself seemed odd, since Longarm knew Chisum and Meriman were on sides irreconcilably opposed to one another.

Meriman spoke under his breath. "Well, we can get it on the road now. Here comes ol' chili con carne and his slutty daughter." His voice rose. "Get the don's baggage aboard, Tom-Tom, and let's head for home."

Longarm watched the Spanish grandee and his daughter cross the sunstruck yard, and caught his breath.

Here were more of the principals in the fight down at Silver City. Four deadly enemies and the presiding judge. Looked as if it ought to be a great trip, these people locked together in a hot stagecoach.

The grandee and his daughter were two beautiful people.

The don carried his huge sombrero, embroidered with bands of real silver and nugget gold, as were his other vestments, from his beige jacket of doeskin to the buckles on his fine tan *zapatos.*

He was a big man, with silver hair that caught and reflected the sunlight. His face was the color and texture of old gold, his black eyes large and commanding. His features were sharply hewn; he had the look of the tenth-generation aristocrat. The most striking thing about him, though, was his graceful, pantherlike stride. He seemed to move effortlessly, gliding across the sun-braised ground as if he owned it and this whole corner of the universe.

But the man's daughter was the one who really caught Longarm's eye. She moved as if dancing to unseen marimbas. In her lace mantilla and ankle-length muslin walking dress of bright Spanish print, she gathered all light and air and fire.

There was a radiance about her, from her rich black hair caught with combs, to her silver-tipped slippers winking as she glided beside her distinguished parent.

Her brows arched daintily over almond-shaped, olive-black eyes. Her light golden flesh gleamed as smooth and unblemished as Spanish polychromed tiles. Her features were delicately cut, except for her full-lipped, sensuous mouth.

Her throat was a slender column, and her low-cut, lacy bodice accented the golden rise of full, high-standing breasts. Her waist was no more than twenty inches around, and her hips measured precisely the same as her bust, Longarm swore inwardly.

Longarm watched them approach, awed in spite of himself. The daughter seemed not to see them standing beside the coach; they simply didn't exist in her world. The father saw them, but showed no enthusiasm. He held his regal head erect, faintly aloof and withdrawn, without being discourteous. He was, in fact, icily polite. The *gringos* could expect nothing more from them.

Their servants stowed their baggage atop the coach, while the don supervised silently. Then he smiled faintly at his daughter and nodded toward the coach. She smiled back and gathered her skirts above her ankles when he touched her elbow to help her enter the tonneau of the carriage.

11

"Señor Salazar. Señorita Salazar." Meriman's voice stopped them. "Meet our other passenger, Mr. Custis Long. Don Hernán Jorge Cortéz Salazar and his daughter—I regret, Doña Fernanda, I don't know *your* full name."

"Doña Fernanda Maria Louisa Carlotta Salazar," Don Hernán said in a barely civil tone, still gently touching her elbow. "If you will permit us to enter. *Gracias.*"

Doña Fernanda settled herself in the plush seat facing forward at the other end of the seat where John Chisum sprawled, head back, eyes faintly amused. Her father sat between them, rigid, as if at attention.

Meriman winked at Longarm and swung up into the coach. He sat facing Chisum. Longarm got in beside Meriman and found himself gazing directly into Señorita Salazar's black, deep, unaware eyes. She stared through him, around him, over and past him, but he never once caught her even covertly looking *at* him.

Tom-Tom slammed the door, folded up the metal step, and levered himself up on the boot. The coach rocked gently for a moment and then rolled out of the yard as if riding on velvet.

Longarm sank back, luxuriating after the cramped torture of the old stage south from Denver. Without invading Doña Fernanda's space, he could stretch out his legs. He exhaled heavily, hoping against hope for a quiet trip.

From the moment the coach pulled out of Socorro and headed west, they could see the Black Range like a fringe of jagged black turrets. Once in a while, a white streak would shoot upward through the black faults. These were the only breaks in the high-flung formation. Not a tree or any vegetation showed on the high tors of those barren granite peaks. A few places were shattered at the head of a stream, or black crevices ripped through the forests of fir, spruce, and pine at lower levels. Or, infrequently, a snow-capped peak wore a yellow-leaf aspen like a single jaunty feather.

"Looks barren, don't it?" Meriman nodded toward the distant hills reared against the vermilion sky. "But I can assure you, Mr. Long, from Cookes Peak all the way north—one hundred and twenty-five miles in length and twelve miles across—that's the richest danged ground on the face of God's earth."

Something tapped against Longarm's boot and he jerked his head up, certain that Doña Fernanda Salazar had kicked him covertly, as if they shared some secret joke on the millionaire mine operator.

The ceramic-glazed smoothness of that lovely face remained aloof, remote, unaware of him.

He exhaled, chalking up the faint tap of the silver-tipped slipper as accidental. But now he was more aware of her than ever, able to yank his gaze from her, but not his heated thoughts.

"Had a few killings in Grant County over the last few months, Longarm," John Chisum began.

"And there will be more, Señor Chisum." Don Hernán Salazar's chilly, precise voice slashed across the rancher's.

"There have been a few cases of fellows letting daylight through one another in downtown Silver City," Meriman said, shrugging. "Don't mean anything—just a couple of citizens full of tarantula juice."

"It's more than that, and you know it, W. W.," Judge McLoomis said. "Silver City is unlike most mining towns—or always was, until now. It was built by men who meant for it to last, not to turn into another ghost town like Shakespeare or Chloride. These killings have been cold-blodded and premeditated—and most of them have been committed by hired, professional gunslingers."

"Nobody has been able to prove that, Judge," Meriman said in his mild voice.

"It will be proved," Judge McLoomis said. His voice was restrained, but quavered with suppressed emotion.

"Maybe you have some interest in these killings, Longarm?" Chisum suggested, watching Longarm narrowly.

"Don't know anything about all this." Longarm saw that this dialogue was like something planned to draw him into the discussion of the bloody troubles erupting in the mining town. It was the quickest way they knew to find out which side of the fence he was on. One thing certain: he was caught between two mortally opposed camps in this plush carriage.

Longarm shrugged. "Like I say, none of this is in my bailiwick. Unless some government official is killed, murder is a local matter."

Don Hernán nodded his leonine head. "As it should be, *señor*. As it should be. The federal government refused to help us when Grant County wanted to annex itself to Arizona. We asked then only to be freed from domination by the Santa Fe Ring. Washington would not aid us then, let them keep their hands off now."

Longarm nodded. He knew that the Santa Fe Ring, although long since broken, hadn't yet died in the memories of many who lived in these parts. In fact, the last time he'd been in New Mexico Territory, he'd come down to follow up a suspicion that the notorious Ring had been revived to extort money from the new railroad that was laying track west from the territorial capital. At this moment, however, he decided to keep his mouth shut and listen to what the others had to say about it, and maybe pick up a few clues as to exactly how the sides in the present matter were being drawn up.

"What the don refers to is—" Judge McLoomis began.

"Ancient history," Meriman said.

"The Spanish Grant titles," Judge McLoomis continued. "All this country was once part of Doña Ana County. Doña Ana, according to Spanish maps, included all land west of the Rio Grande to the California line. This included all the territory acquired by the United States in the Treaty of Guadalupe Hidalgo in 1848. Creation of the Arizona Territory in 1863 cut off all of Doña Ana County west of the thirty-second meridian, and those of us in what has become Grant County wished to annex ourselves to Arizona to escape the Santa Fe crooks, who are held in certain special interests' pockets. Let's say the people holding Spanish titles figured they'd fare better as part of Arizona Territory—"

"A sad fact which has been demonstrated a hundred times, proving that we were right," Don Hernán cut in. "We wanted to escape dishonorable and greedy exploiters. And we sit now at the mercy of rapacious mining interests—men who kill us when we protest their greed."

"Now just a cotton-pickin' minute, Don Hernán," Meriman said, grinning coldly in a way that made him look sinister and deadly behind his smiling. "We miners are just businessmen like you. Businessmen trying to get along. That's all."

14

Again, that silver-tipped slipper bumped lightly but surely against Longarm's sensitive instep.

His head jerked up. There was no mistaking the touch. He wore low-heeled cavalry stovepipe boots that were more suited for running than riding, and he paid extra to have them made of soft calf's leather because he spent as much time afoot as he did in the saddle; these boots were lightweight and comfortable and fit him like a second layer of skin. Also, the road was level, the ride smooth, with little jostling compared to ordinary conveyances.

His mouth sagged slightly. When he glanced at Doña Fernanda, he found her serene face expressionless and bland. She seemed unaware of him. And she seemed, too, to have collected all the light in the cab about her. Even the gold cross on its fragile golden chain about her throat glittered and winked at him.

Holding his breath, Longarm decided to play her game. He inched his boot over and laid it gently against her slipper. Her reaction was instantaneous. The tiny foot was yanked away, though the gorgeous face remained cool and impassive.

Longarm withdrew his foot. Hell, he was too old to play footsie with a girl, anyway. He was a federal lawman, not a callow youth. He would put the aloof *señorita* out of his mind. He liked women, and she was the loveliest of females. But he wasn't desperate, not even for a magnificent nymph like this. To hell with her.

He was aware that a heated, though carefully modulated and courteous argument was raging between the four men.

Strange as hell! Getting odder by the minute. These four men, he knew, were principals in the violent belligerence brewing, boiling, and bubbling in the cauldron of Chloride Flats. Yet these disputants—whose very lives depended on the outcome of this struggle—kept their voices civil and restrained— a hell of a lot more civilized than the statesmen wrangling over per diem in the Colorado assembly.

"The New Mexico Territorial Legislature must pass the Anti–Hydraulic Mining Act. *En nombre de Dios,* they must," Don Hernán said emphatically.

"They will," Chisum said with cool certainty. "Hell, it's the

15

only kind of protection that will keep you Grant County ranchers and farmers in business."

Meriman laughed. "Gentlemen, gentlemen. A little reason. Please. There's no chance of that law's passing, now or later." He put his head back, laughing. "The law's evil, discriminatory, and unconstitutional. And as long as I've got a dime left to buy me some politicians, I'll hire the best that money can buy—and I'll fight you people for my constitutional rights."

"*Your* constitutional rights, W. W.?" Judge McLoomis said in a mild, sad tone. "What about the rights of others?"

"They'll have to get some crooked politicians and protect their own rights," Meriman said, laughing.

"That's a very cynical charge to make, W. W.," the judge protested. "Not every politician is crooked."

"Maybe not." Meriman smiled and shook his head. "But all of them I've ever met are for sale. Usually the price is right, so I can buy the best. And that's why, gentlemen, I guaran-damn-tee you that your blasted Anti–Hydraulic Mining Act won't get off the floor."

"It had better," Don Hernán Salazar said. "Or you miners will face an uprising of outraged ranchers and farmers and decent ordinary people that will make nightmares of your best days."

The atmosphere crackled with tension inside the swank coach, but Longarm, remembering what Marshal Billy Vail had said when he assigned him to this case the other day in Denver, knew that right had to crouch, scared to lift its head, somewhere between these two bellicose camps.

And then, suddenly, he felt that soft, insistent pressure of a slipper against the inside of his boot. It was hard to think about Billy Vail, or even to care about Billy Vail, with that kind of action going on.

He sucked in a deep breath and gazed across the seat toward Doña Fernanda. The lovely lady gazed quietly out the window, seemingly entranced by the sun-blasted wasteland of cactus and sage.

Chapter 2

"This here Silver City mess is a touchy thing," Billy Vail said. The Chief U. S. Marshal, First District Court of Colorado, was balding and going to flab from being saddled too long at his government-issue pinewood desk. At least fifteen years older than Longarm, Vail still had the old hardness in his muscles, face, and eyes. He wore ill-healed scars like proud badges from long-ago violence in almost forgotten hellholes.

"I'm waiting for the assignment you give that ain't as touchy as saguaro cactus, Billy." Longarm sank deeper into the red morocco-leather chair and stretched his long legs out in front of him. Idly he watched his boss paw through the paperwork that flooded in from Washington, all of it marked "urgent."

As Billy continued to ponder, Longarm took a cheroot from his coat pocket and glanced disinterestedly up at the banjo clock on the paneled wall behind Vail's high-piled desk.

He let his gaze pass over the austerely government-issue-furnished office and thanked God he wasn't desk-tethered in here like poor Billy Vail. There was no carpeting because Vail's pay grade didn't rate a rug. There were exactly three chairs and two filing cabinets. A single window opened on the plaza. A thirty-eight-star American flag shared wall space with a map of the western half of the United States and a framed photograph of President Hayes. How in God's name did the poor devil stand it cooped up in here eight eternal hours a day?

Longarm watched Vail from slumbrous eyes. Hanging around Denver for any length of time got him itchy and nervous. He was ready for a new assignment, but he wasn't sure he liked the sound of Billy Vail's voice when the chief marshal repeated, "Real touchy."

Longarm flicked the head of a sulphur match with his thumbnail and lit his cheroot. "You mind telling me what's so all-fired sticky?"

"We don't get many like this," Billy said. "This fight is between two sets of decent people. Probably as honest, law-abiding, and God-fearing as people anywhere. Good-hearted, open-handed, do anything for you. But right now they're all set to kill each other—and you got to stop 'em."

"I'm a deputy marshal, not a preacher."

"You won't get nowhere in Silver City preaching sermons. Preaching a sermon is fine. But first you got to get somebody to listen. These people have already proved they're through listening to anybody or anything—except their own sixguns."

"Sounds like this is something that's been smoldering for a long time."

Billy Vail glanced up and nodded. "Just what this here report says. You ain't already seen it, have you?"

"Hell, Billy, I don't read half the reports you hand over to me. I ain't ever going to read 'em uninvited."

"What you got is no ambition," Billy Vail said. "Don't you ever want to better yourself?"

"I consider myself bettered every time I escape this office and get all the way out of Denver."

"You ought to feel bettered to hell, because you're going down to the Black Range country of New Mexico. Lot of trouble down there. Hired guns and other lawless characters drifting in, invited, sent for, or just looking for a quick buck. Added to everything else, they got Indian trouble."

18

"Oh, hell. I thought nearly all the Indians down thataway had been pacified by this time."

"Things are quiet most everywhere by now, but down there they've put some prideful Apaches on the same reservation with Indians they feel nothing but comtempt for. They won't stay. And being Apaches, they raise hell and scalps every time they break loose."

"That's for the army, not us."

"That's part of what's rankling on the Grant County people. They've appealed to General Hatch and Governor Wallace, and they've written directly to the War Department in Washington, and all they get is a runaround. And they're sick of it.

"And they got the smeltering plants and hydraulic-pressure hard-rock mines that are poisoning all the creeks, rivers, and wells, killing cows and people. And they're sick of that, too."

"Does that bend any law that we can bend back into shape?" Longarm inquired.

Vail shook his bald head. "Not that I know of. Now the cattlemen have brought in hired guns to ventilate any silver people sent out prospecting."

"That break any federal laws?"

"*And* they got a hot election coming up. Two factions. Two sets of candidates. And both factions willing to kill people rather than let them vote against 'em."

"That sounds like a territorial matter."

"Right. I'm just telling you what's got these people so all-fired jumpy. This indignation against the army, the legislature at Santa Fe, and each other has been building up for years. Ranchers are threatening to war on the miners unless the legislature passes laws restraining the miners. Mining people say they'll blast the ranchers to kingdom come if that law does pass."

"I admit, it does sound touchy. Sticky. Dangerous. Explosive. But what's it got to do with us?"

"Just one little thing," Billy Vail said with a briar-eating grin. He looked as if he sat across a poker table, ready to play his ace. "Some of the holdings down there are part of the old Spanish grants, protected by a U. S. treaty with Mexico. Prospectors and miners have been moving in on this land, and the county officials are backing up the miners."

"And that's a federal offense," Longarm said.

Billy Vail nodded. "You got it."

Longarm felt the brief, insistent pressure of Doña Fernanda's dainty slipper. He decided to ignore her. Only she wouldn't let him. Bump. The toe of her slipper hit his boot. Again. Again.

He stared right into her face, forcing her to meet his gaze. He said in a loud, cold tone. "Sorry my feet are so big, ma'am. I know they keep bumping you."

Don Hernán looked alarmed. He gazed first at Longarm as if undecided whether to kill him or ignore him. He glanced at his daughter. "Would you like to trade places with me, my dear?"

She spoke blandly, as if Longarm hadn't spoken, as if, in fact, he didn't exist. "I'm quite all right, Father. Thank you."

She returned her gaze to the view beyond her window. But suddenly something struck the instep of Longarm's boot, fiercely and sharply.

He sat back, grinning, and said nothing.

Longarm listened to the four men arguing. They were like duelists. Thrust, parry, dodge, lunge. There was much to say on each side. The only trouble was, these men had said it all to each other hundreds of times. Everybody was talking and nobody was listening.

Letting his gaze touch idly at them, he decided he could not figure any way to settle the war between them, short of letting them kill each other off and start again.

He grinned crookedly. Sounded like a good idea, except he knew from talking to Governor Wallace that this option was entirely unacceptable, though the governor admitted he considered it in those moments when he was tired enough.

Lew Wallace had kept Longarm waiting in the outer office of the Governor's Palace at Santa Fe less than fifteen minutes. He got up from behind his littered desk and came around it smiling, ramrod-straight from his years as army officer. Now in his fifties, Wallace had served as a junior officer in the Mexican War. Then he'd practiced law until he entered the

Union Army during the Civil War, when he was promoted to the rank of major general. He'd been governor of New Mexico Territory for the past four or five years, and he was getting itchy, exasperated with some of the bureaucrats he had to deal with, about ready to move on.

"Longarm," he said. "I'm truly pleased they sent you down here to help me again." He smiled in an ironic way. "I'd have asked for you, but I knew better. You ask directly for what you want, and some bureaucrat gets his tailfeathers up and spends time and money figuring why something other than what you want would be much better for you."

"Sounds like you're at last beginning to learn what it's really like, trying to work for the government," Longarm said.

"Oh, I've known those sad and disillusioning facts for a long time. I tell you, Longarm, I can tolerate anything except stupidity, and that's what I encounter every day of my life— present company excepted, of course."

"That's why it's refreshing for me to get out and deal with everyday folks, General—train robbers, highwaymen, high-graders, cattle thieves, fugitives—your ordinary voter."

Wallace put his head back, laughing. "It does my heart good to talk to you, Longarm. I've been asked to serve as U. S. ambassador to Turkey. How would you like to go along as my deputy? We could have some laughs."

"Thank you, General, but I got all the laughs I can stand right here—in English. Might take me a while to learn to laugh in Turkish."

Wallace grinned. "Well, you think it over. Do us both good to get away. I thank God I'm going. There'll be just as much trouble in Turkey, but until I learn the language, I won't know about half of it. Now you take this mess down there in Grant County—"

"That's why I'm here, sir."

"I know. And I don't envy you. I'm pleased they sent you; you did a fine job the last time you were down this way." He grinned and shook his head. "But I sure would appreciate a mite less noise this time, son."

"I don't think there'll be much noise," Longarm said. "Because I don't think there's any answer."

The governor frowned. "Oh, there's got to be. I never saw so many really good people so godawful dead wrong and pigheaded in my life. Why, I've had decent, upstanding people from Silver City stand right here in my office and accuse me of accepting bribes."

"Ranchers accusing you of selling out to the mining people?"

"That's right. But the next man up is a miner, and he's ready to impeach me for selling out to the ranchers."

"You do need help."

"I imagine we all do, from time to time." Wallace exhaled wearily and passed a hand across his forehead. "I'll tell you, Longarm, even though I'm looking forward to that ambassadorship, I'd a whole lot rather be able to just sit down and finish my book."

"You're still working on it, huh? I reckon it must be nearly done by this time."

Wallace smiled. "Just about. It needs a little polishing, that's all. Writing a book can be a lot like fighting in a war, Longarm—harder in some ways. I think *Ben Hur* is the last one I've got in me. In a funny way, I don't even care whether anybody likes it or even reads it; it needed to be written and I wrote it, and I can't tell you how it's changed my life."

"I don't know about anybody else," Longarm said, "but I read books from time to time, and I look forward to getting it."

"You'll have to let me know what you think," Wallace said. "About this present business, though—I'm afraid you're going to be pretty much on your own. I don't have too many friends down there. The ordinary people have been hammering at me for troops to protect them against renegade Apaches, but we just don't have them. The miners don't trust me. The ranchers think I've sold them out. Most of the local politicians are as crooked as they accuse me of being. If you get in trouble, it might not do you much good to call on me."

Longarm reached out and clasped the governor's shoulder. "Don't you worry about me, sir. I'm used to working alone."

He turned around and headed for the door, fixing his Stetson on his head as he crossed the floor with long strides. Just before he reached the door, Wallace called out to him:

"Longarm?"

The tall deputy turned. "Yes, sir?"

"God bless you, son."

Longarm wanted a smoke, but figured it was hot and close enough in this carriage without the smell of his cheap cheroot. He fumbled one from his pocket, bit off the end, stuck it in his mouth, and chewed on it.

"Hope you don't plan to light that thing up," W. W. Meriman said, making a face.

"That nickel cigar will bring Indians," Chisum said. "They'll think it's smoke signals."

"I'd appreciate your not jesting about Indian attacks, Señor," Don Hernán said. "There is no point in upsetting my daughter."

"Besides," Longarm said, "this is no nickel cigar. They're *two* for five cents."

For the first time he saw a response in the *señorita*'s face. She smiled. It was faint and fleeting, but it was a smile. "It's all right, Father," she said. "I am no more nervous about Indians than the rest of you."

"Apaches are on the warpath," Chisum said. "There's no sense in denying that."

"You know why, don't you?" the *señorita* demanded. Her lovely, faintly accented voice had music in it, even when it was vibrant with outrage. "It's all the fault of the same federal government that leaves us without hope against the mining interests."

"Surely, ma'am, you ain't ratin' me alongside them murdering Apaches?" Meriman said.

"If I have," she replied, "I apologize—to the memory of Mangas Colorado."

Far from being insulted, Meriman put his head back, laughing. "Now, you really are a spirited little filly, ain't you, ma'am?"

"I know right from wrong," Doña Fernanda said in a cold voice. "I know the Department of Indian Affairs has handled the entire matter of the Apaches stupidly."

"Would you let them run free, ma'am?" Meriman baited her, amused.

"They run free anyway, don't they, Mr. Meriman? They are killing people between here and the Arizona border with

23

Mexico. Maybe if the U. S. government weren't so stupid, that killing could be avoided."

"I'd be interested in knowing your remedy, Señorita," Judge McLoomis said. "I must confess. To my mind, dying by Indian torture must be the most hideous death possible. They won't simply let you die—man or woman—they must torture you to death."

"That will be enough, sir," Don Hernán said, sitting straighter and gripping the head of his cane. "Quite enough."

"My apologies, Miss Salazar," the judge said. "You mind saying what the U. S. government has done wrong?"

"It hasn't done anything *right*. An example of the stupidity of the government and the army can be found in the capture of General Crook. That poor deluded man, surrounded by Apaches, went out *hunting* to prove to them he wasn't afraid of them. Well, poor stupid man, I imagine he was afraid of them before they were through with him.

"And that's the way the government has dealt with the Apache. They could have shown better judgment in the first place than to move the Chiricahua chiefs from the Mescalero agency and from their old hunting ground. That was bad enough. In the Apaches' eyes, it was unforgivable. But the Great White Father had hardly begun to mistreat the Apache. The government moved the Chiricahua to the San Carlos Indian Agency in Arizona. Here the proud, arrogant Apache, who never bowed to any man on earth, was expected to mingle with what they considered the dogs of the Tonto ranges. The insult was more than the Apache could endure. They nursed their anger, and they broke out, just as Washington must have known they would."

"There is one solution for the Apache problem. Right or wrong," Meriman said. "The only way is to convert them."

Doña Fernanda sat forward, trembling. "You would kill them all?"

Meriman smiled at her, teasing. "You got any better notions, ma'am?"

"I don't agree with W. W.," Judge McLoomis said.

"You never do," Meriman taunted the magistrate. "The day you agree with me is the day I know I'm dead wrong."

"I don't agree we should slaughter the Apache. They are

brave, honorable men, and probably the best warriors the world has ever known." The judge exhaled heavily and shook his head. "But our stage roads and our railroads and our outlying ranches and farms must be made safe—somehow."

Meriman laughed. "Did I ever tell you people how I traveled the stage roads and was never bothered by Injuns or highwaymen? And me carrying ten thousand dollars in silver at the time." He slapped his knee, laughing.

He faced them, letting his smiling gaze touch each of their faces in turn. "I decided to get married. This was some years back. The roads were lonely and infested with thieves who'd kill you for your horse, money, or shoes. But my lady lived in Santa Fe—and that was no easy or safe trip at the time. I bought myself a medium-sized Bain wagon. I put in silver bullion in bars to the amount of ten thousand dollars. Then I built me a false bottom over this, so as to allay suspicion of my load. Tom-Tom hitched a four-mule team and we took along a young fellow who could handle a gun. We set out on the road to Santa Fe. We were not molested along the entire route. Nobody dreamed we were carrying silver. We got to Santa Fe in time for the wedding. And I felt so good that after the ceremonies were over, I gave away the whole ten thousand—every penny of it. And it was money well spent. My lady was the most gentle of women, God rest her soul."

The coach rounded a curve on an uphill grade and Longarm was thrown suddenly forward by an abrupt, lurching stop.

W. W. Meriman cursed a blue streak, apologizing to Miss Salazar between every fiery word. He yelled, "What the hell's the matter up there, Tom-Tom?"

Meriman slapped his door open and leaped out to the ground without bothering to lower the metal step. He'd no sooner struck the roadside with both feet than he braced himself, his mouth sagging open, his eyes stretching wide, and both arms reaching for the sky.

"Looks like a holdup, Mr. Meriman, sir," Tom-Tom said from the driver's seat.

Abruptly a tall man appeared, carrying a double-barreled shotgun, just beyond Meriman, using the mine owner as his shield. The robber wore a floppy-brimmed bonnet, its brim sagging down over his face. His features were concealed behind a brown bandanna, and his clothing was covered by a knee-length smock made of Pride of Denver flour sacks sewn together.

Instinctively, Longarm drew his Colt .44-40 from its cross-draw rig. The Colt's barrel was cut off to five inches and there was no front sight. He didn't want—at times like this!—the revolver's barrel catching in the open-toed holster made of waxed and heat-hardened leather.

As he moved to draw, Don Hernán Salazar moved just as instinctively. The grandee leaned forward, reaching out as if he meant to wrest the gun from Longarm's grasp. In fact, Salazar's dark hand did close on it firmly.

"Put that gun away, Señor," Don Hernán ordered between clenched teeth. "No possessions any of us carry upon his person is worth starting a gunfight that would endanger the safety of my daughter."

From outside the coach, the highwayman laughed and nodded. "The old greaser is right, you men. You fellows play it smart, you step out easy, with your hands on top of your heads. And don't make no moves that'll get lead to flying. I warn you, I got four trigger-happy fingers on shotguns fixed on you people from the underbrush. Now, out! Get out here!"

Swearing and moving awkwardly, John Chisum stepped out to the roadbed. He locked his fingers together atop his Stetson, but he swore loudly about the indignity. "No decent man is safe on the road anymore."

"And you ain't either, John Chisum." The robber laughed, jerking his gun and ordering Chisum to stand a couple of feet from Meriman, where he could watch them.

Longarm holstered his gun reluctantly, conceding that the aging Spanish grandee was right. Whatever the thief wanted, it was probably only money.

He watched Doña Fernanda move past her father and step out of the tonneau. Meriman moved to help her, but the robber yelled at him warningly and Meriman straightened, standing unmoving.

Longarm found his only pleasure in the situation watching Doña Fernanda's *caderas* undulate in time to that unheard Latin fandango.

Don Hernán followed his daughter and stood protectively

near her, closer than the robber wanted, but finally even he relented to Salazar's parental instincts.

Judge McLoomis stepped out of the coach, clasping his hands on top of his derby. The crook laughed tauntingly. "Well, Judge, I do believe you and me have met before."

"Next time we meet," McLoomis said, "I'll sentence you to hang."

"Be careful how you talk, Judge. You ain't in your court-room now," the thief warned.

Longarm was last to leave the coach. He kept his hands as far as possible from his gun, and then, when he straightened on the roadway outside the carriage, he locked his fingers on top of his head. This amused the robber. "Funny, big fellow, you don't look half tough like that."

Longarm shrugged, watching the gunman and glancing about the roadway and brush alongside it.

The highwayman had the situation under control. The men from the coach stood limply, as if all the starch had sweated out of them. Tom-Tom slumped near the big steel-rimmed front wheel, his face twisted in a disgusted look of defeat.

Longarm gave the thief good marks for choosing the ideal site for a stickup. At this point the incline was steep enough to slow the horses, with the coach straining upward between huge boulders. They were already above one thousand feet, and at this altitude scrub oaks, evergreens, alders, and mountain maples grew thickly along the roadway. Dry creekbeds were the only break in the thick brush, like escape routes winding in dozens of directions, uphill and down.

Longarm watched every move the highwayman made, trying to find something about him to remember, a clue to his identity that he could use later.

He shook his head. There was little. Under the floppy-brimmed old hat, the fellow wore one of those shaggy Toby wigs from the traveling stage shows that were beginning to fan out from the Midwest. This hair hung, like a poodle's bangs, like a shabby shade to within a quarter of an inch of the mask. Eyes were always a good clue, but this hombre had concealed his perfectly.

Longarm inhaled deeply, and held his breath. One fact was becoming clear: the robber seemed to know these people. He'd laughed at Meriman's complaining, calling him by name. He'd taunted the judge, recalling earlier meetings, and he'd called John Chisum by name.

This was no spur-of-the-moment holdup. Obviously it had been well-planned. Even this told Longarm something about the crook, as did his six-foot height, and his horse, a dappled, gray-faced mustang ground-tied just ahead of the coach. It was the kind of horse that was easy to lose in a small herd.

Longarm's mouth tightened. Whoever this hombre was, he knew the stage and its schedule, and seemed aware of who its passengers were.

With the shotgun's hammers back, ready to fire, the robber passed before his captives like a general in some military review.

"Now, I'm going to deal with you people one at a time. You cooperate, nobody gets hurt. First, I want each of you gentlemen to throw your guns onto that bullhide at my feet. Don't be in any stampede to obey me, but don't try to hold out on me—that could be bad for your health. Savvy?"

Meriman carried a small revolver with a pearl-gray handle. He placed it on the bullhide and straightened. Chisum was next. He hesitated and finally withdrew an old but well-kept hogleg from its holster and tossed it on the ground.

"Once you git that cannon out of drydock, I bet you're a killer, ain't you, Chisum?" the robber taunted. The rancher didn't bother to answer him.

Tom-Tom, frustrated, tossed his sixgun to the ground. Judge McLoomis shook his head. "I don't carry a firearm," he said.

The robber stood before the magistrate, shaking his head. "I swear, Judge, you ain't real smart."

The judge shrugged, but said nothing more. The don's gun was small, carried in a half-sized leather holster. Don Salazar tossed it disdainfully upon the bullhide.

The robber paused in front of Doña Fernanda. "You got anything hid away, Señorita?" he teased.

"Let my daughter alone, sir," Salazar said.

"You forget, Mex. I got the gun."

"If you touch her, I'll kill you."

The highwayman sucked in his breath and stood for a moment, gazing from under that comic wig and floppy brim at the Spanish rancher. Then, deliberately, he reached out and yanked the gold cross and chain from Doña Fernanda's neck, shoot it in his fist, and pocketed it. Doña Fernanda winced, but remained unmoving.

The robber faced her father again. "'Listen to me, greaser. You make one move and you're a dead spic. You hear me?"

Salazar straightened and stared straight ahead, as if facing a firing squad. He said nothing.

The thief moved on to Longarm. "Throw your gun over there, big fellow. Slow and easy."

Longarm tossed his Colt to the bullhide. The robber waited, then raged. "That ain't all hombre. Put the little hideout in the collection. Fast. Move fast."

Longarm blinked, surprised. How did this character know he carried a derringer in his vest pocket at the other end of his watch chain? This whole business grew odder by the minute. He unclipped the little double-barreled .44 derringer from the chain, hefted it in his palm, then tossed it to the ground.

"That's better," the thief said. "You don't want me losing my temper. I get mad easy and I don't forget quick." When Longarm didn't answer, the highwayman said, "You can start. Throw your money on the ground."

Longarm withdrew the few greenbacks from his pocket.

The thief grabbed the money, thumbed it, and laughed in disdain. "That all the money you got?"

"I work for a living," Longarm said.

"Well, that ought to tell you something. I tip bartenders more'n this." He motioned with the gun. "You got a wallet?"

Longarm removed his wallet and identification from the inner pocket of his frock coat.

"What's that?" the robber said.

"My badge, identification, and orders," Longarm said.

The crook nodded. "I'll just take all that."

Reluctantly, Longarm surrendered his papers, badge, and identification. He watched the robber pocket his belongings and step past him.

"All right," the highwayman said. "You people get the idea. I want your money and your valuables." He threw a croker sack beside the bullhide. "Just toss everything on the ground. If you got any personal trinkets you want, keep 'em. I don't want them."

Meriman's wallet was fat with greenbacks, and the thief

laughed in satisfaction, pocketing it. Tom-Tom moved to hand over his money, but the robber shook his head. "Keep your money, Tom-Tom. I know old W. W. don't pay you decent wages."

Don Hernán Salazar's wallet was Mexican-made, of silver-ornamented calf's hide. The highwayman removed the money from it and tossed it back to the grandee. "Keep it, greaser. I wouldn't be caught dead with it. Besides, it would tie me to this job—and we don't want that, do we?"

Judge McLoomis carried only a few more dollars than Longarm. The thief took it. "Holy Mary, I don't see how you law people live on what you make. You ought to get on the take, Judge. Hell, even crime pays better than *this.*"

Even with the shotgun fixed on his bellybutton, old John Chisum was reluctant about handing over his money.

The robber's voice raked the rancher. "John Chisum, you old miser. Get busy and hand over your money, pronto. Savvy? I don't want to hang around here all day on account of you. We can put buckshot in you, and take what you got."

Chisum threw some greenbacks at the robber's feet. The masked man raged. "Come on. Fork it over."

Chisum's head jerked up. "You've got all I have on me."

The robber's hands trembled on the shotgun. "I know you're lyin', you bastard. You just take off that money belt you got around you. And do it quick."

Chisum stared at the masked man, stunned. "How'd you know I wear a money belt on me?"

The robber didn't answer, just motioned with the gunbarrel for the rancher to speed it up. The cattleman hesitated a long beat, then unbuckled the money belt and threw it on the ground. "There, damn you!" Chisum raged. "Money paid me for my cattle. There's ten thousand in that belt."

"Thanks, John," the bandit said. "I knowed it."

He secured the top of the sack, then knelt and tied the corners of the bullhide together. Hefting it all, he backed away. "I'll leave you gents' guns about a mile down the road. Look for the bullhide, Tom-Tom."

He retreated to his horse, mounted, and then yelled back, "By the way, Meriman, don't fret about them shotguns in the underbrush. I work alone, you old mulehead."

Chapter 3

Silver City owned the first swaybacked main street that Long-arm had ever seen.

He stepped down from the coach outside the two-storied Exchange Hotel, said to be the largest in the territory, and stared in amazement at the washed-out avenue. For almost the full mile of its south-sloping length, the narrow thoroughfare was like a trough between sidewalks and buildings rearing back on both sides.

The town squatted in a sump of pines, junipers, and live oaks, on a chloride flat. To the north rose scarred hills, dotted with thousands of raw-looking stumps. Once those hills had been thick with every kind of tree, but by now, prospecting and lumbering were shaving them bald. Beyond those foothills rose totally barren mountains that were the color and texture of elephant hide, wrinkled and scaly, above shattered mesas.

The exhausted team pulled into town in the middle of the morning following the robbery. They'd spent the night at the stage stop in Hillsboro. They'd been accepted as guests of W. W. Meriman's charge account, since he was the only one known to be affluent enough to be trusted by the unsympathetic hostler.

The trail started winding through dark hills upward to the seven-thousand-foot elevations of the Continental Divide, which crossed the towering Mogollon, Pino Alto, and Mimbre ranges to the tablelands and the grassy mountain meadow.

The coach lumbered down out of the eastern hills bordering the mud flats and dense with groves of cedar and pinyons, to the level mesa luxuriant with grama grass, tall sunflowers, and countless tules in the marshes that the Mexicans had long ago named *La Cienega de San Vincente*.

The town had grown rapidly and sturdily in the twelve years since John Bullard discovered silver in the Chloride Flats area about three miles west of what was now the town site.

An incredibly substantial small city, with the sedate brick-and-stone look of a New England town about it, had been surveyed and laid out. Because law demanded that a town site be created before a mining claim could be validated, Bullard's people had requested a site one mile in each direction from the spring at which Indians had watered their stock, and around which they'd made camp since time immemorial.

Longarm was shocked to find there were no longer even any traces of those first brush shelters, liberated Civil War military tents, and slab-sided structures of the first boom years. For all its apparent stability, this town had been constructed hastily and not with great wisdom. For one thing, the houses had been built close together along each side of narrow streets that turned into torrential, flash-flooding arroyos in rainy seasons.

Those narrow streets were crowded, and the stagecoach had to worm its way through them. The town was busy and loud. The roaring of quartz mills and smelting furnaces reverberated into the hills and echoed back; the noise had long ago driven out the last antelope and deer.

Out of the gorge below town and past the five busy mills, rose the din of thunderous stamps pounding away at the precious ores taken from the mines. The deep, continual boom of the hard-rock blasting in the hills, the clatter of huge mule and ox

32

outfits fighting their way through the congested streets, the raging of muleskinners, the bellowing of oxen, the braying of mules and burros, and the hammering of carpenters added to the raucous skirmishing that erupted spasmodically from any one of eight saloons.

The passengers rode silently, each seething in his own way about the daring robbery.

Longarm bit back his rage. As far as he could determine after turning the matter over and over in his mind, this holdup had two definite targets: his badge and identification, and John Chisum's overloaded money belt. All the rest was somebody's window-dressing.

Somebody had set up this welcome for him. That somebody knew who he was, where he hailed from, and what his business was in Grant County. John Chisum's ten grand was icing on their cake, too good and too easy to resist.

And this bold bandit, in his flour-sack smock and Toby wig, belonged in Silver City. Longarm was betting his life on that, whether he wanted to or not. He wouldn't recognize that arrogant crook, but the gunman knew *him*—as would the badman's bosses.

Longarm was the first out of the coach, but he saw that his bag was buried under the others' luggage on the roof rack. Neither the passengers nor Tom-Tom seemed in a rush to debark, though John Chisum had whined about nothing but reporting that robbery to Sheriff Henry Whitehill the minute he hit town. There was nothing to do but wait.

Sighing, Longarm leaned against the big steel-rimmed wheel and idly studied the strange concave street and the buildings crouched precariously along it.

People hurried on both flag sidewalks. Two men fought tiredly outside the O. K. Saloon; idlers whittled in the overhang shade in front of Miss Nellie Pyles' Fandango House. A piano rattled in the St. Julian Bar. Nearer, scavenging hogs snuffled in the curbside refuse outside a bakery across Main Street from the Exchange Hotel.

Longarm glanced around. Strange to find hogs wandering loose in the downtown of such a modern-looking metropolis. But no stranger than the washed-out street, so uneven that people walking along it moved with a short-legged, loping stride. And no stranger than Indian smoke signals puffing against the sky from not-too-distant hills.

His gaze touched at the only man in Silver City besides himself who seemed totally without a goal or occupation. This fellow, rail-thin and rangy, with a flat-crowned planter's hat, a faded pongee shirt with sleeve gaiters, and whipcord pants over scuffed riding boots, leaned against the jamb at the double-doored entrance of the Exchange Hotel lobby.

The fellow seemed to be looking at nothing, interested in nothing. Yet each time Longarm checked, he appeared to jerk his gaze away, toward a sheep-trailed cloud, a cottonwood tree with a blackbird jawing in it, or the hogs snuffling in front of the bakery. But he showed no concern for anything, not even the boar who grunted and jerked up his head, refusing to move for pedestrians or horses.

Longarm didn't even know the word *paranoia,* but this was the feeling he fell victim to. Everything appeared stacked against him—the robbery and the thief who had taken his badge and identification, and now this fellow, too damned disinterested, in the shade of the hotel veranda.

There was something more than vaguely familiar about that lantern-jawed face, the coyote-thin shanks. A bell rang deep in his mind. The answer leaped like a grasshopper and he couldn't pin it down. But he'd seen that jasper somewhere and the associations were none too pleasant.

At last the other passengers decided to leave the coach. Don Hernán Salazar and his daughter were the first to alight.

Doña Fernanda looked through Longarm, neither speaking nor admitting his existence. It was as if she'd never seen him before, and if she had, she couldn't bother to remember where. The shared ride, the robbery, the secret pressure of her silver-tipped slippers? These things had never happened, said the bland expression in her serene and lovely face.

"Goodbye, Señor," Don Hernán said. "I hope God will help you to see the right, and once you see the right, you will use your power to help that right prevail."

"It was good making your acquaintance, Señor Salazar," Longarm said. "If my work brings me in contact with you and your *rancho,* I sincerely hope we fight on the same side."

"Vaya con dios." Salazar wrung his hand, then touched his

34

daughter's elbow and they went around the stage and across the flag walk to the hotel veranda.

Judge Lynch McLoomis was next. He gave Longarm a wan, hesitant smile. "I'm not a wealthy man, Mr. Long, nor really a very influential one. But if there is any way I can help you while you're in Silver City, I hope you'll call on me."

Longarm grinned. "Sure, Judge. Us poor but honest hombres have got to stick together."

Tom-Tom handed down the judge's scuffed suitcase, and the magistrate stepped up on the walk and hurried away in the bright sunlight.

John Chisum swung down from the coach, slowly and awkwardly. He met Longarm's gaze and swore fluently. "It isn't arthritis plaquing me, Longarm, it's losing ten thousand goddamn dollars."

Longarm grinned. "I know how you feel, Mr. Chisum. Always hits me the same way."

"I worked hard for that money." John Chisum clenched his fist. "I'm on my way to start a fire under Henry Whitehill's tail. I know they won't catch this crook, but by God they're going to hear my report."

Tom-Tom handed down Chisum's bags. The cattleman jerked his head toward a Mexican boy lounging on the walk and told him to take the bags into the lobby. "And carry 'em careful." John Chisum started around the coach. "You don't break nothing, *muchacho*, I'll give you a whole dime."

Longarm sagged against the wheel and watched Chisum limp past the loiterer at the hotel entrance. Chisum didn't give the critter a glance, and the fellow quickly lost interest in the passing rancher.

Longarm figured that damned near half an hour had passed since Tom-Tom parked this rig before the Exchange Hotel. Time didn't mean much to these people, evidently. Tom-Tom yelled for porters, who came and carried Meriman's bags into the hotel lobby.

Meriman shook Longarm's hand and grinned. "Just recollect, Mr. Long, when you're choosin' up sides in this fracas, us miners was here first. This is our land. Without us, there wouldn't be nothing here but San Vincente's swamp. A man digs something out of this hard rock. It don't set easy when

35

somebody—even Uncle Sam—tries to take it away from him. Savvy?"

"I'm not choosin' up sides, Mr. Meriman. I work for the U. S. government. Long as you're breaking no federal laws, you got nothing to fear from me," Longarm said.

"Oh, I don't fear you. Or the U. S. government. Reckon God had plumb run out of fear when my turn came. Or maybe I'm too dumb to be scared. I know what's mine, though. And I mean to protect it. But remember this too, later on, Mr. Long. I ain't attempted to bribe you. Others may try, but not me. I got a lot of respect for you. But respect ain't got a damn thing to do with fear."

Longarm heard Tom-Tom call his name from the roof rack. "Here's your bag, Mr. Long."

"Throw it down, Tom-Tom."

Tom-Tom lifted the bag to heft it over the side of the coach when something along the street snagged his attention. Laughter and taunting yells went up.

Longarm turned and followed the direction of Tom-Tom's gaze. He saw a beautiful young Mexican girl—somewhere in her teens, beautifully put together, and still growing, her breasts and hips and thighs straining against the fabric of her faded cotton dress. But even barefoot and outgrowing her frock, the *señorita* was prettier than a green chili pepper, and much hotter looking.

Men yelled and whistled and called propositions from the shade of buildings, but she ignored them. She carried a large wicker basket of washed clothing atop her head, gliding along and carrying her weight on the small of her lithe back, as graceful as a ballet dancer.

"Some hot tamale," Tom-Tom said. He tossed down the bag and Longarm caught it.

As he turned to go around the coach, he heard a low-throated rumble in front of him. He looked down and found a tusked boar set solidly in his path, head lowered, beady eyes fixed on him.

Longarm took a step forward and the boar growled again, like a vicious dog ready to attack.

"Why, you son of a bitch," Longarm said. "Everybody else in this town can walk around you, but I'm damned if I will."

36

He stepped directly toward the hog. As the snarling animal lowered its head, Longarm brought his boot toe up into the boar's throat.

The hog grunted and backed away, head still lowered, but no longer aggressive. Longarm stepped around him and moved toward the walk when somebody yelled across the street and a woman screamed.

The boar, enraged, was charging toward the Mexican girl. Men yelled advice and shouted at the boar, but nobody moved to help her.

Her eyes staring, her mouth round, the Mexican girl stood transfixed in the middle of the street.

Looking around, Longarm grabbed up an adobe clump. He took three steps forward and hurled the rock-hard mass at the boar. It caught the animal behind the ear and jerked its head around, two feet from where the girl stood immobilized by panic.

In the precise instant that the boar swung its head toward him, Longarm dropped his arm, drew his gun, and fired.

The report rattled along the street. The bullet struck the boar between the eyes, and the animal staggered slightly and then toppled on its side at the washgirl's bare feet.

Unable to speak, the Mexican girl stood unmoving, her face frozen in terror.

Louder, for that instant, than all booming and battering and clattering sounds in Silver City, the explosion stopped all activity. Then the crowd spilled from the walks into the ditchlike middle of Main Street, and ran toward Longarm, the girl, and the dead porker.

Shoving his gun back in its holster, Longarm picked up his leather bag and walked out to where the girl was turned to stone.

"Are you all right?" Longarm said.

The girl started, as if awakened from a dream. A shudder wracked her body. She tried to smile and failed. She looked around, confused, as if unsure even where she was.

At last she was able to think and act again. She tilted her head, steadying the basket of clothes atop her black mass of hair. *"Sí, Señor.* I'm all right now. Thank you. *Gracias."*

Her great olive-black eyes were fixed on his face, and she

nodded anxiously, but did not take her gaze from him.

"You need any help, carrying that load wherever you're going?"

"*No Señor. Gracias. Gracias. Gracias.*" She stared at him, attempting a pale smile. Even as she walked forward again, stepping around the dead hog, she continued to impale him with those incredible eyes. "*Gracias.*"

People stepped back, making a path for the girl. They stared at the hog, at Longarm.

"That's some shooting."

"Never saw a quicker draw than that."

"Who'd you come to town to work for, mister?"

"You going to work for the ranchers or the miners?"

"That's some slick draw."

"Man, that was fast."

Longarm merely shook his head. As he turned toward the hotel again, a small Mexican urchin, in torn red shirt and ragged knee-length pants, caught at his coattails.

"*Señor.* Mister. Please, sir."

Longarm paused, staring down at the brown child and the four or five like him who suddenly seemed to sprout from the infertile ground of the street. "Yeah?"

The child smiled and nodded toward the dead boar. "You through with that there hog, Señor?"

He studied the sunflower faces turned up at him hopefully. He grinned and nodded his head. "All through."

"Can my friends and me have him?"

"I sure as hell don't want him."

"It is all right then for us to take him?"

"What are you going to do with a big old boar like that?"

The child nodded his head emphatically. "We'll eat him, Señor. By golly, we'll eat him."

Another boy grinned, nodding. "We'll roast that sumbitch on a spit over a pit fire—"

"We feed everybody on our street, Señor. Big fiesta."

"We won't waste nothin', Señor."

"We use everything about that old pig, 'ceptin' his whistle."

"You got him," Longarm said. "How you expect to get a boar that sized home?"

"You watch us, Señor. We pretty strong fellows."

He grinned, watching the children clutch the boar by curly tail, hooves and head, bent over, half-dragging, half-pushing it along the sandy street.

Turning, he saw that the loiterer was no longer in the Exchange Hotel lobby doorway. He shrugged his jacket up on his shoulders, thinking he'd have to get a wire off to Billy Vail. Held up. Robbed. No badge. No identification. No money. Help! Hell of a way to begin a new assignment. . . .

"Friend. You want to hold it right there, friend?" The voice kept addressing him as "friend," but Longarm found nothing cordial in the flat, challenging tone.

Still headed toward the hotel, he turned his head and winced. The loiterer had found himself a goal. It looked like a robbery in broad daylight. He stared at the gun and grinned coldly, "Sorry, friend, you're too late. I already gave."

Suppressing that nagging sense that he knew this ugly face from somewhere, Longarm shrugged and moved away again.

"Unless you want a bullet in your back, friend," the man said, "you best stand right where you are."

By now the crowd on the street had glimpsed this byplay in front of the hotel. They gathered in a wide half-circle, staring.

Angered, Longarm hesitated. The man thrust the gun butt with such force into Longarm's kidney that he gasped for breath.

Speaking over his shoulder, his voice low and deadly, Longarm said, "I don't know what your game is, but you better back off. I've already given you twice the time I usually allow scum like you."

"Just stay where you are, man. I'm Deputy Town Marshal Wheeler, and you are under arrest."

Longarm stared at that lean and hungry face, feeling rage rising in him along with the increasing certainty that he knew this man.

Deputy Town Marshal Wheeler showed Longarm his badge pinned on his pongee shirt, and tilted up his gun.

Longarm said, "You mind saying why I'm arrested? I haven't even spit on the sidewalk yet. Hell, I haven't even *gotten* to the sidewalk yet."

"You're under arrest for carrying a gun inside the town

limits. And for firing said weapon in a public place, endangering the lives and safety of citizens. You want to come quietly?"

"Hell, no. I just got into town. I wore my gun into town." He grinned, remembering the way the bullhide had been left on a boulder beside the stage road about a mile from the scene of yesterday's holdup.

"I don't want to argue with you, mister. I'm just telling you, you're under arrest. You been in town at least a half an hour. I seen you when you come in, and you was armed then. 'All persons except officers of the law are required to remove their firearms within twenty minutes, upon their arrival in the limits of settlements, cities, towns, and school districts.' That's a territorial law."

"I'm a federal law officer," Longarm said.

"All you got to do is prove that."

Longarm stared at the deputy. Proving his identity wasn't going to be easy. Common sense dictated that he go along with the arrest and clear it up at the town marshal's office; that should be easy enough.

He shrugged. "Fair enough. Where you taking me?"

"I'll tell you what you need to know."

Longarm stared hard at the deputy marshal. "You're some tough character, ain't you, Wheeler?" And suddenly he remembered where he had seen that face.

Setting himself, Longarm swung around. He brought the leather case up with all the strength he could put behind it, into Wheeler's crotch.

The deputy fired his gun, but the bullet sailed harmlessly toward Mars. He dropped the pistol, gagging, and bent over, clutching at his belly, trying to vomit.

People gathered closer, yelling at each other. Longarm drew his gun and held it at his side. "You people just stand quiet, this is between the deputy marshal and me."

He set the bag down and holstered his gun. Catching Wheeler by the nape of his neck, he held him wriggling like a fish at the end of his arm. He removed the deputy's handcuffs from his gunbelt and pulled one arm behind Wheeler's back, snapped on the cuff, then caught his other wrist in the second link.

Holding the deputy by the manacles, Longarm looked at the stunned crowd. "Where's the law office?"

"Jail and town marshal's office, they're over on Hudson Street."

"Where's the sheriff's office?"

A teenaged youth stepped forward. "I'll show you, mister. Sheriff's office. That's at the County Building, over on Broadway."

"All right." Longarm handed his leather bag to another boy. "You take that bag in to the clerk at the hotel desk there. You tell him it belongs to Deputy U. S. Marshal Custis Long—and that I said he's to hold it until I get back."

"Yes sir, Marshal." Beaming with pride and self-importance, the boy ran across the walk and up the steps, going across the shaded veranda and into the hotel lobby.

"All right," Longarm said to the teenager. "Show me the way."

"Hold it," Wheeler gasped. "I ain't going nowhere . . . I'm in pain . . . I need a doctor . . . I can't walk."

"You'll walk, or I'll drag you," Longarm said. He shrugged. "It's all the same to me."

Chapter 4

Playing pridefully to his audiences along the walk, the boy shouted, unnecessarily loudly, over his shoulder. "Sheriff's office is just ahead, Mr. Long. I sure am proud to be able to help a United States Federal Marshal. Yes sir. Name's Binky Waters, if you need me anytime again. Yes sir."

Longarm grinned. "Thanks, Mr. Waters. You've done a great job."

"Shucks, Mr. Marshal Long, you can just call me Binky."

The Grant County Building was an imposing two-story brick structure dominating a busy street. Binky Waters held open the front doors for Longarm. Wheeler would have fallen to his knees, but Longarm caught him by the belt and yanked him upward. The town marshal screamed in renewed pain.

"You either get used to that hurtin', old son," Longarm told him, "or you get used to going where I point you."

Wheeler tried to curse him, but he was in too much pain to speak. Binky Waters held open one of the double doors to the sheriff's suite of offices. Longarm shoved Wheeler into the room ahead of him.

One man, middle-aged, hatless, wearing a denim shirt, suspenders, and a deputy sheriff's badge, sat at a pinewood desk facing the front door.

"Good God! Wheeler!" the deputy sheriff said. He got up from his chair. "What in the name of God's going on here?"

"Never mind Wheeler," Longarm said. "Where is the sheriff?"

"Sheriff Whitehill ain't in just now," the deputy said.

"When *will* he be in?" Longarm asked. He threw Wheeler into a straight chair against the wall. Wheeler hit the chair a glancing blow, but toppled to the floor. When Longarm made no move to help him up, Wheeler writhed painfully until his back was against the wall, and then he crouched there, his legs drawn up, his face contorted.

The deputy sheriff stared at Wheeler, agonizing on the floor. He said, "Sheriff ain't often in these days. What's going on here?"

Remembering his stolen identification papers, Longarm dug two bits from his pants pocket and tossed it to Binky Waters, who caught the money, grinning. "Binky, you think you could find Judge Lynch McLoomis and ask him to come down here? Tell him Custis Long regrets troubling him, as tired as he must be, but he might need him."

"Sure, Marshal Long. Know right where Judge McLoomis lives. I'll sure do that." He darted from the room, slamming the door so hard behind him that it trembled in its frame.

The deputy came around the desk. "Why don't we just slow down and back up here. Tell me what's going on."

"As you can see, Deputy—"

"Len Hazelton—"

"I'm Deputy U. S. Marshal Custis Long, First District Court of Colorado—"

"You mind showing me some kind of identification, Mr. Long?"

Longarm looked into Len Hazelton's sun-weathered face and faded blue eyes, trying to find some hint that the sheriff's deputy knew—as Town Marshal Wheeler had clearly known—

that he had no identification. But the deputy's simple face concealed nothing. He looked like an honest lawman doing his job. Longarm hoped so; it would be a hell of a thing if the sheriff's office turned out to be mixed up in the Spanish land grant thefts.

Longarm spoke rapidly. "We'll get to that, Hazelton. If I'm not who I say I am, all you got to do is let Wheeler go, and nobody's hurt. If Wheeler is who I damn well know him to be, I want him arrested."

"Hold it! Hold on there! There you go, getting your damn cart ahead of your horse again. Let's take this slow, Mr. Long. You say your name's Long?"

"That's right. Custis Long. Deputy U. S. Marshal—"

"I heard that part. I ain't trying to make trouble for you, Mr. Long. But I ain't knowingly making any trouble for Sheriff Whitehill's office, neither. In the first place, I don't know what your charge against ol' Slim Wheeler here is, but no matter what it is, it looks like a local town matter to me."

"Well, take my word, it's not."

"Something for the town marshal's office, Mr. Long. Town Marshal Herm Tuttle gets all misdemeanors and felonies inside Silver City town limits, Mr. Long. You did say Long, didn't you?"

"That askin' me my name is gettin' just a trifle old, Hazelton. My name ain't the problem here."

"Might be to me," Hazelton said in a flat voice. "I ain't seen a badge or identification. This here is a sheriff's office, Mr.—"

"Long," Longarm said.

"We go by the book. That's all. Like I say, I think you better take your charges to the town marshal's office, over at the city jail on Hudson Street—"

"Not this time, Hazelton." Realizing he was still holding his Colt in his fist, Longarm shoved the gun back into its cross-draw holster and wiped his sweaty palm along his skin-tight brown tweed pants. "As you can plainly see, this here varmint *is* a town marshal—"

"Yeah. I know Slim. But I ain't satisfied about who you be, Mr. Long."

Wheeler stirred on the floor, pressing his fists against his fiery abdomen. He spoke in grunts. "Make the son of a bitch prove who he is, Len."

At this moment the door to the sheriff's private inner office was pulled open, and John Chisum limped through, his face livid with rage. "Sorry, I can't help overhearing this damfool wrangling out here. I'm trying to write a report that the effing sheriff ought to be in his office to *hear*—and I have to listen to you make a goddamn fool of yourself, Len. This is Marshal Custis Long, from Denver, just as he told you. We had a little holdup trouble on the way in to town from Socorro, and lost all our papers and all our money. But that doesn't change a thing. Custis Long is who he says he is, one of the best, most decent lawmen I ever crossed trails with. And if you're so anxious not to make any trouble for Sheriff Whitehill's office, you'll cooperate with Mr. Long right down to the last dotted *i* and crossed *t*. You got that, Hazelton?"

"Thanks, John," Longarm said, grinning at the fury in the rancher's tone.

Chisum shrugged. "Any time, Longarm. One thing I can't stand is stupidity, and this goddamn office reeks with it." He turned, stalked through the doorway, and slammed the door again.

Some of the starch had melted from Len Hazelton's rigid spine by now. He watched Longarm with a hangdog look, his face down.

Longarm spoke in a flat tone. "All I want, Deputy, is a look at your wanted fliers. That's all."

Hazelton nodded, subdued. He jerked his head and Longarm followed him to a polished pinewood table pushed against the wall and stacked high with papers, orders, and arrest reports. Hazelton picked up a six-inch-thick pile of fliers and handed it to Longarm. "It's just that we don't want no trouble with the town marshal's office right now," Hazelton said in an apologetic tone.

Longarm was already flipping through the file of wanted criminals. The face and the flier he sought burned clearly in his mind. He shrugged and spoke over his shoulder. "But you don't want any trouble with the U. S. marshal's office, either."

Hazelton leaned against a filing cabinet, his arms folded

across his chest. On the floor across the room, Wheeler agonized, writhing, his handcuffs scraping the paneled walls. A lonely fly sang the blues around a brass spittoon.

Longarm's hand closed on a flier and he yanked it from the file. "Here he is. Knew I recognized the son of a bitch."

At that moment the front door of the sheriff's suite was thrown open and two men charged in. The man in front was of medium height, pot bellied, flashily dressed in Mexican boots and a Mexican shirt with patch pockets, and packing a low-slung gun. The second man was taller, leaner, harder, and more professional-looking. The man in front yelled, "What's going on here?" He spotted Wheeler trussed up on the floor, and yelled, swinging his arms, "What in *hell* is going on here?"

Holding the wanted flier, Longarm glanced toward the harried and gaudy man in the doorway. "I'm from the U. S. marshal's office in Denver. I just arrested this jasper on the floor."

"Now just a minute," the gaudily dressed man said. "You're talking to the law here. I am Town Marshal Herman Tuttle. Now let me see some kind of papers or badge or something that proves who the hell you are."

Longarm's voice dripped sarcasm. "I think you damn well know, Marshal Tuttle, that I don't happen to have any identification on me."

Tuttle's face flushed red to the roots of his hair. He jerked his head around, confused for a moment, and then straightened. "Just what kind of accusation is that, mister? I don't know you. I know nothing about identification, except that I want to see some. And fast."

Len Hazelton spoke in a flat, warning tone. "He's who he says he is, Herm. I think you better go along with him."

Herm Tuttle sputtered like a boiling kettle, then went over to the chair beside which his handcuffed deputy was sprawled. He took a key chain from his belt and knelt beside the fallen man.

"I wouldn't do that, Tuttle. You're in trouble enough without aidin' and abettin' this jasper any further."

Tuttle lunged up and heeled around. "What in hell are you talking about, mister? What the hell you mean, coming into this town and makin' accusations against me and my deputies?

What the hell have you done to poor ol' Slim?"

Longarm's cold voice mocked the marshal. "Pore ol' Slim ain't 'Slim' nobody. His name ain't Slim Wheeler, in case you don't know. This character's name is Dippy Dan Watson. Wanted in ten states at least, for every felony they got a name for in the law books. But the latest outstanding warrant on him is this one. Less than a year old. Five hundred dollars reward for him from Wells Fargo—for robbery."

The town marshal looked stunned, but he didn't do it very well. He may not have been much of a town marshal, but he was one hell of a poor actor.

Longarm managed not to tilt an eyebrow. He had this pot-bellied bastard's number. He'd known about the stolen badge and identification, and Longarm was just as sure Tuttle knew Slim Wheeler's real name; maybe he'd known it when he hired him.

"His moniker ain't Wheeler," Longarm said. He tried not to laugh at the hypocrisy that filled this room as thick as smoke. "Here's his picture, his real name, some of his aliases, some of the charges against him."

"Ol' Slim Wheeler?" Tuttle said, shaking his head. "Why, I can't believe that."

"Can't you? Among other things, they call good ol' Slim the Orphan Maker, 'cause he'd as soon shoot women as men. Don't you ever check on men before you hire 'em?"

Tuttle sucked in his breath, puffing up like an adder. His face flushed red. "Just what are you accusing me of, sir?"

Longarm shrugged. "Well, for starters, Marshal, how about hiring gunslicks like ol' Slim here as your deputies?"

The town marshal looked at his own deputy and at Hazelton, but didn't look at Longarm as he raged, "You just watch your tongue, mister. You don't know what the hell you're talking about."

"I'm talking about Dippy Dan Watson. Orphan Maker Watson. Wells Fargo thief. Gunslick. Walks in and you hire him—as a deputy marshal. His own flier ought to be in your wanted file. It took me less than ten minutes to find it in *these* files. And yet you didn't even bother to check."

"You listen to me. I'm an honest man. An honest man. I'm no crook. You can't accuse me of being a crook."

48

"Crook or stupid." Longarm shrugged. "Take your choice." He was aware of the brief exchange of glances between Hazelton and Tuttle's deputy.

"Goddammit, you got no right to accuse me. I never stole a penny in my whole life. I try to keep this town honest. I make a mistake, and you want to disgrace me! I hired Slim Wheeler in all honesty, taking his word he was what he said he was. I never knew about him robbing no Wells Fargo, and my hiring him don't prove I did, and you can't tar me with the same brush as him!" Tuttle was trembling and his voice shook.

"I hate to call such an upright lawman a liar, Tuttle, but you are full of horseshit. I walk into town, and this thief tries to arrest me. I slapped him like I would a fly, because I knew what you should have known when he walked in your office. He's a wanted fugitive with a price on his head."

Tuttle tried to smile. He shook his head and swallowed. He said in an uncertain voice, "You a bounty hunter?"

"Now what in hell is that supposed to mean?" Longarm asked threateningly.

"Nothing! Nothing! I was just thinking. If you are a federal marshal, like you say you are, then you can't collect the reward on ol' Slim—I mean on the man you call Dan Watson."

"That's right. I can't collect rewards."

Marshal Tuttle nodded, satisfied. "Then you won't have no objection, should I file for the reward. Eh? I mean, you can't collect it. A town marshal don't make all that much that five hundred bucks won't come in handy."

Longarm gazed at the marshal until Tuttle looked down at the floor, face flushed. Longarm laughed. "You know, Marshal, I'd have bet you'd decide that was the best way to handle the matter of ol' Slim."

"Well, long as there is a reward, I don't see why I can't benefit. I mean, Slim come in here and lied to me. Made trouble for me. Made my office look bad. Make you call me a crook. I ought to get something out of it."

Disgusted, Longarm shrugged and turned his back. He said to Len Hazelton, "Got an empty cell? I want to put Watson in it. And I want to be damn sure he stays there."

Worried, Hazelton glanced toward Tuttle. "We'll hold Watson for you, Marshal Long, sure. But for how long?"

"You just *hold* him, Deputy," Longarm said wearily, "on a federal warrant. I'll get word to Denver and they'll send marshals down here for him. Here's the rundown on him—his own picture on his own private flier. He's guilty as hell. Hold him."

Exhaling heavily, Longarm laid the wanted flier on the deputy's desk. He glanced at the lawmen and nodded curtly, striding toward the door.

Tuttle's voice stopped him like a dally-welty. "Just a minute, Mr. Long. You mind saying where you're going?"

Longarm heeled around. His gunmetal eyes blazed, but he kept his voice flat. "You got your own goddamn trouble, Tuttle, without worrying about me. Where I'm headed right now is none of your goddamn business."

Suddenly the town marshal spoke in a very different tone, oily and self-satisfied. "Well, now, just a minute, Mr. U. S. Marshal. I reckon I *am* the law inside the Silver City town limits. I ain't oversteppin' my authority one whit if I ask you to accompany me and Deputy Tyne here" —he jerked his head toward the serious-looking individual who'd followed him into the sheriff's office—"over to *my* office on Hudson Street."

Longarm set himself, legs braced apart, and stared at the town marshal. "You mind saying why?"

"Well, great goodness, Mr. Long. Just a routine matter. Just a courtesy of one lawman to another, you might say. I got to have a report on my deputy, that's all. I thought you might be willing to answer a few questions."

Longarm was getting tired. It was one hell of a stage ride southwest from Denver to this sunny little suburb of hell. The people he'd dealt with so far in this self-styled "diamond city of the hills" had exhausted him further. The little game Town Marshal Herm Tuttle and Deputy Town Marshal Eastwood Tyne were playing angered and fatigued him almost past the point of endurance. He held a built-in hatred for dishonest law officials; they gave the whole job a bad name. And these fellows were not only devious, they were as stupid as stumpknockers.

The game they played for the folks who crowded the streets between the County Building and the marshal's office and jail

50

on Hudson Street was called Looking Important, Official, and Dedicated.

Though neither Tuttle nor Deputy Tyne had guns drawn, and though Longarm's Colt still rested in its holster, the town marshals managed to make this procession look to their constituents like an official arrest.

The crowds parted as they walked east along tree-lined Broadway. Broadway, running east and west, was wider than Main Street, and was crowded with brick buildings and heavy ox and mule traffic. Some of the men called to Marshal Tuttle, asking what was up. But the marshal only shook his head and looked wise.

Longarm was now aware that the stupid town constable was wise, all right. Tuttle and Tyne knew he'd been set up, his identification stolen. Wheeler had been sent to arrest him and bring him in, and if he hadn't slapped Wheeler like a horsefly, he'd have been in the marshal's cell now, cut off from any chance of getting identification. Jesus, how stupid could they get?

Stick around, kid, he thought in exasperation, *and find out.*

The marshal walked close beside Longarm, but a step behind him. Tyne plodded in their wake, and without looking over his shoulder, Longarm knew the deputy had his hand on his holstered gun. It was bad enough working with *honest* stupid lawmen, but to play games with these knaves was asking too damned much. He felt himself drawn tighter than barbed wire in a freeze.

The Silver City jail and marshal's office was a thick-walled adobe-and-pine structure with notched cedar roofing. Tyne and Tuttle marched Longarm into the cramped front office. The building was a long narrow room, partitioned by iron bars. A barred door between the crowded office and the lockup was closed, locked, and chained. The cells beyond it yawned empty. All windows were iron-barred, and even the front door was reinforced with iron.

The front office held five flat-top desks and one rolltop pushed as close together as possible to allow for swivel chairs at each.

Tyne went to one of the flat-top desks and seemed to lose

51

interest in Tuttle and Longarm. He slumped in his swivel chair and didn't look at them.

Tuttle sat down behind the rolltop that had been shoved to one side against the wall, where it was hemmed in by gun racks and hat stands. One almost got the feeling that the deputies had shunted Tuttle off into a corner and that the marshal was too dense to realize it.

Longarm held back a yawn that was equal parts rage, fatigue, and exasperation. He said, "All right, what about these questions? I want to get out of here."

Tuttle glanced up. "Well, Mr. Federal Lawman, if that's what you call yourself, you'll get out of here when I say you can go."

Longarm's hand touched at his gun, but he realized his mistake. Tyne, whoever he had been before he showed up at Silver City and became a deputy marshal, was greased lightning with a gun.

Tyne spoke gently from behind Tuttle. "Just take your gun out real easy and lay it on Marshal Tuttle's desk."

Longarm said, "I've dealt with some stupid shitheads in my time, but you bastards refuse to learn. This is the United States government you're shittin' with."

Tuttle grinned at him in satisfaction. He took up Longarm's Colt, hefted it a moment, opened his desk drawer just enough to slide the weapon in it, then closed it and stared up at Longarm.

Tuttle said, "Mr. Long, what you can't seem to get through your head is, I'm trying to do you a favor."

"Well, quit doing me favors and worry about your own ass, Tuttle. You fellows are gettin' your tails in slings."

"Maybe we are, maybe we're not," Tuttle said in a smug tone. "We're doing our job."

"You mean you're following orders," Longarm lashed out.

"Now just hold on there."

"Hell, you must have *some* reason for what you're trying to pull, Tuttle."

"I have, Long. My duty to the good people of this here township. That's all that's in my mind. You've come in here with accusations, trying to make out I'm less than honest because I hired on an ex-criminal—"

"An *ex*-criminal? Watson?" Longarm laughed helplessly.

"Could be he was trying to go straight. For all I know, he was. I pride myself on my memory, Mr. Long, and if I ever seen any wanted fliers on Slim—or Dan Watson, as you call him—I plumb disremember."

"Why don't you give me my gun back and I'll get out of here before I arrest you and your whole damned crew?"

"For what?" Tuttle shouted, trembling.

"We'll just shake you all up together in a net and see what falls out of the wanted fliers. What you got? Five deputies? I'll give you odds there are wanted posters on every damned one of them."

"Now you listen to me. I'm telling you for the last time, I'm an honest man, sir. I got no connection with any crimes Dan Watson may have committed, or any gunslicks he may have known. I'm doing my job, that's all I'm doing. I'm doing my job."

Longarm shook his head wearily and said, "Look, Tuttle, I'm too tired to argue with you. Give me my gun and I'll get out of here. I'll be in town. You got maybe forty-eight hours to clean house, fire your criminals, or get out of town yourself. I'm telling you for your own good. But I don't intend to stand around and watch you rats run."

Marshal Tuttle's face blazed red. His eyes narrowed, widened, then narrowed again. His mouth sagged open and then screwed into a tight line. He looked as if he might suffer a stroke on the spot. It took him a long time, but finally he got himself under control.

"Now you listen to me, Long, or whatever in hell your name is. I got you in here for one reason: to advise you, for your own damned good, to get out of Silver City, out of Grant County, and—if you know what's good for you—out of New Mexico."

"Listen, you silly shit. Don't threaten me."

"I'm telling you for your own good. It was bad enough before. Poor ol' Slim was ordered just to bring you in so I could talk to you. But, oh no. You had to put on a show. You had to make me look bad. You had to arrest Slim—with his own cuffs. All right, big man, let's see what it buys you."

"I wish to God I knew what you're talking about, Tuttle."

"You! Dammit! You. You arrested Slim Wheeler. It wasn't bad enough you came in where you wasn't wanted or needed! No, you had to arrest Slim." Tuttle shook his head. "Slim has got friends."

"I doubt that."

"You're about to find out, mister. Slim has friends in *high* places." Tuttle shook his head, looking ill. "Why, he was put on my staff at the request of—of mighty high-placed folks."

Longarm gazed across the desk at the sweating lawman, and shrugged. "I don't doubt that. I reckon every deputy you've got was handed to you by folks in high places. It's the easiest way to keep their hired professional guns in town—and wearing guns. So let's stop kidding ourselves about Slim's friends in high places. I've got friends in high places—in the United States Department of Justice. And if you think getting rid of me will solve your problems or Slim's problems or the problems of Slim's friends, you're even stupider than you've sounded so far. Why, you poor bastard, if you don't clean up this office, the Justice Department is going to be on your ass like ducks on a june bug."

Marshal Tuttle hesitated. He touched at the papers on his desk, then glanced at Tyne, slumped behind his desk across the room. "Does that mean you're not going to take my advice?"

"What advice is that?"

"To take the next stagecoach out of here. Your fare will be paid. Any destination. Any direction. You stick around, you're going to get your head blown off."

Longarm shook his head and said, "It wouldn't help any, you silly clown. If your friends get rid of me, the Justice Department will send four more just like me—and ten more, and twenty more, until your asses are wiped plumb clean. If that's your bosses' message to me, this is my message to them. Shape up or get out. Killing me won't buy them anything but a hang-rope at Leavenworth."

Tension crackled in the cramped office. Longarm stared down at the marshal until Tuttle lowered his gaze, his trembling fingers shuffling papers impotently in front of him.

Longarm glanced toward Tyne. The deputy appeared to be napping, but Longarm wasn't foxed. He'd seen gunslicks like Tyne play possum too many times to be fooled. The only thing he could figure was that these idiots thought he was as stupid as they were proving themselves to be.

He exhaled heavily and backed toward the door. His movement put both Tyne and Tuttle in his line of vision and in front of him. "That all you got to say?" he asked Tuttle.

"That's all, except I know what you're up against. So, God help you."

"Well, just give me my Colt and I'll mosey. You tell your masters that I'll be here in town, and if they come for me, they better come armed."

The marshal shook his head. "I'll just hang on to your gun, Long. At least until you come up with some kind of acceptable identification. You don't wear no gun in this town until I *know* who you are."

"Going to send me out to face ol' Slim's friends unarmed, eh, Marshal?" Longarm inquired.

"You're in this mess on your own, dammit. You had no call to come into this town and stir up trouble."

"I'll give you two minutes to hand over my gun," Longarm said.

This bold statement even amused Tyne. Both the marshal and his deputy shared a hearty laugh. Longarm let them laugh. Hell, probably a long time between laughs in a business like theirs.

It wasn't until they stopped laughing that they noticed that Longarm was patiently holding a compact, double-barreled derringer trained on them.

"You son of a bitch!" Tyne raged. "They *told* you he carried a hideout!"

"Toss your gun over here, Tyne," Longarm said matter-of-factly.

The disgusted deputy slid his gun across the floor. Longarm knelt and took it up. "Now yours, Tuttle. You're safer not carrying one anyway."

"That's Christ's truth," Tyne said between clenched teeth.

Longarm made Tuttle unlock the barred door to the cell-block. When the marshal and his deputy were inside, he turned the key, removed it, and locked the chain. "Looks good on you," he told them. "Try it on for size. I think you're both going to have to get used to it."

"You son of a bitch," Tyne said. "I didn't care before, but now you've made *me* look bad. This is a personal thing, Long. Me and you. I'll be coming for you, and don't you forget it."

"Let me know when, I'll bake cookies," Longarm said. He retreated to Tuttle's desk and pulled open the big drawer.

"You stay out of my drawer!" Tuttle yelled.

Longarm stared down at his Colt, and his gaze struck his own wallet in the corner of Tuttle's messy desk drawer. Longarm felt something slip downward in his belly. He'd known Tuttle was stupid and dishonest, and that Tyne was likely a professional gunslick with a record longer than his prick. But it was still a shock to find his stolen belongings in the town marshal's desk. It looked like conclusive proof that the marshal was in cahoots with the bandit. In fact, the bandit could have been one of Tuttle's deputies.

He should have felt triumph, but he didn't. Rotten lawmen made him sick at his stomach. They likely always would, no matter how many he ran up against.

He spoke casually. "You wanted some identification, Tuttle? Here it is. Papers that identify me, and very likely are going to convict you."

Chapter 5

Miss Nellie Pyles was the first woman Longarm ever saw smoking in public. Oh, he'd known a few ladies who smoked privately, and he'd seen backcountry women sucking on clay pipes, and Mexican women puffing on cigarillos, but here was a lady sitting on the main street of town in her Sunday best, dragging on a fancy, ready-made cigarette, as unconcerned as a puppy lapping hot milk.

When he walked into the Western Union office next door to Miss Nellie Pyles' Fandango Saloon on the swaybacked Main Street, the lady sat rocking on the shaded veranda of her smart-looking brick structure, wreathed in a cloud of gasper dust.

He wrote out a brief report on the robbery and state of affairs in Silver City and requested Billy Vail to send him a hefty expense-account advance, unless he wanted a U. S. employee to sleep in an alley and work on an empty stomach. In his mind's eye he could see Billy swearing as he read this telegram, but he also hoped he could see him sending funds by answering wire.

When he emerged from the telegraph office, he paused on the flag walk in the sunlight. The smoking lady was still there, drumming nervously on the arm of her rocking chair with her inch-long, red-lacquered fingernails.

She was only a few feet from him, in the shady spot of her banister-enclosed veranda. Music and laughter and the tinkle of glass emanated from the batwings beyond her. She seemed oblivious to these noises of commerce, either from the patrons of her saloon or from the clattering of the telegrapher's key in the Western Union office next door.

She gave him a warm, friendly, and uncluttered smile. She waved her cigarette and stopped her constant fingernail tattooing for a moment. "Howdy, Marshal," she said.

Longarm's brow tilted. "Howdy, ma'am. How'd you know I was a marshal?"

"Ain't much goes on in this town that I don't know. I heard about you. Anyhow, I seen you when you come in on old W. W.'s swank coach. I watched you over there and I said to myself then, I said, 'That's for me.'" She put her head back, laughing. "For a price, of course."

Longarm grinned with her. "Of course."

She drew hard on her cigarette and exhaled a cloud of blue smoke. "Come on up and set a spell. If I like the cut of your jib—or anything else—I'll buy you a drink. Oh, by the way, I own this establishment. My name's Miss Nellie Pyles. Of course it really *ain't*, but that's close enough."

Longarm smiled and vaulted easily over the banister. She watched him, her mouth pulled into an admiring grin. "You look good—and hard," she said. Miss Nellie Pyles seemed to be giving him her full attention, and yet she continued to drum with those fingers.

Miss Nellie Pyles wasn't beautiful anymore as she slunk reluctantly past forty, but about her hung an indefinable aura, the memory and faint aching of true and voluptuous beauty. Her remembered loveliness was in the flawless smoothness of her peach-round cheeks, murrey lips, and tilted jawline. She carried her head proudly on the slender column of her throat.

Her violet eyes were oddly shaped under arched and penciled brows.

She wore a feather boa over a fresh party dress; she would tell you she had to look dressed for a party every day, no matter how hellish she felt inside. Her body was encased and plastered over with layers of fragrant powders and a barrage of perfumes. When Miss Nellie Pyles entered a room, people knew it—for a long time after she had gone.

She snapped her fingers, and when a scantily clad girl came out on the porch, she ordered drinks for herself and Longarm. Then she sat back, lit a fresh cigarette from the butt of her last, and tossed the butt into the street. She sucked in a long breath of smoke and drummed at her armrest with her nails.

Longarm found her puzzling. She appeared to be one of the most self-possessed females he'd ever encountered, and yet she was a chain smoker—in public—lighting one cigarette from the butt of another. And the way she drummed her chair arm incessantly with her fingertips had become an unconscious habit by now, and it could be distracting. Inside, this lady was a bundle of raw nerve ends.

When the pretty young waitress brought their drinks, Miss Nellie toasted Longarm. "Well, here's looking up your old peccadillos, Marshal. I wondered how long before they'd send in a federal marshal to referee the fight."

"The fight?"

"Come on, don't play coy with me. Last time I enjoyed playing coy, I was ten years old behind the barn."

"You got troubles here, all right."

She shrugged. "Bound to have. A town with growing pains. Men wanting different things."

"And wanting them bad enough to kill for them."

"I've seen men kill over the turn of a card."

"So have I. It don't make me in favor of killing."

"I've seen men kill over the turn of a card, Marshal . . ." She tilted her head quizzically. "Long's the name, isn't it?" A wicked smile passed across her features. "Long in name and long in other parts, I'll wager."

Her smile was contagious, and the corners of Longarm's eyes wrinkled as he replied, "Seeing that we're acquainted so intimate already, I reckon you can call me what most of my friends do—Longarm."

Her eyes flickered toward his crotch, then back up to meet his own steady but amused gaze. "Even better," she said. "Anyway, if you want my professional opinion, trouble's bad for business. But there's the other side of it, Longarm..." She paused. "Love the sound of that name...sort of makes me pucker down between my legs."

"In a purely professional way, of course," Longarm teased.

"Of course. A girl's got to live, Longarm, no matter how pretty a fellow looks to her."

"Then I'm afraid we'll have to stay strangers. I was robbed on the way into town."

"Yeah, I heard about that."

"My God, already?"

"Longarm, relax. Things can hardly wait to happen in this town before I hear about 'em."

Longarm grinned. "I'll relax if you will, Miss Nellie." He nodded his head toward her drumming fingers. "That's a pretty distracting habit you got there."

She smiled and stared at her painted nails. "Longarm, a girl's got things bottled up in her—they got to come out some way, or she's liable to go plumb loco."

"I reckon you're right."

"Of course I'm right. I didn't come down all the roads I been down to learn nothing. That's why I'm pleased you're here. Don't know what you can do against so much money and so many hired guns, but maybe you'll get the muleheads to thinking."

"How do you feel about what's going on here in Silver City?"

"How do I *really* feel? I feel men are the biggest damn fools this side of women. They got good things going here. This could be God's country—with screwing at Miss Nellie's as a fringe benefit. But men ain't ever satisfied with a good thing. They got to have it better. They got to have more. And more."

"You mean the miners?"

"And the ranchers." She watched him with an odd smile. "You ain't getting me to take sides, Longarm. I got friends among the ranchers, and just as good friends among the miners.

Friends on both sides. Now the miners, they got money. They don't look so swell, but they're rich as hell." She tapped on the chair arm, smiling.

"And the ranchers?"

"I like cattlemen. Usually a cowboy is a gentler rider on my girls. They don't have as much to spend as the miners, but they do ride in every Saturday night and they're a hell of a lot easier—and cleaner—on the bedsheets."

Longarm finished off his drink and stood up. "It's been plumb refreshing and enlightening talking to you, Miss Nellie. Soon's I get some greenbacks, I'll drop in and buy you a drink."

"You do that, Longarm. And if you need anything upstairs, why, we can run a tab for you. We got every kind of lady a man could fancy, and some even too fancy. I myself offer real interesting variations for special customers, and to me you look *real* special, Longarm." She laughed. "Matter of fact, you sly devil, you've talked me into it. Come on upstairs. One on the house."

Longarm shrugged helplessly. "Miss Nellie, I'm going to have to decline your neighborly invitation. I figure the worst sin a man can commit is to turn down a lady that makes him an offer. But I'm so dog-tired, I want to go to bed alone. Hell, I can't even understand it."

She smiled up at him. "Don't worry about it, Longarm. When you do get a hard-on, and want something different, I'll be here."

Longarm yawned as he walked into the shadowed lobby of the Exchange Hotel. The clerk smiled and nodded as he approached the registry desk.

"Mr. Long? Mr. Custis Long?"

Longarm nodded his head. "I sent my bag in earlier for you to hold for me."

"Yes, sir, Mr. Long. I took the liberty of putting your bag up in your room. We gave you a nice corner room, sir, with cross ventilation and a view of Main Street—"

"If it ain't washed away by morning."

"Been a lot of rain and floods and mud, Mr. Long, but it's still there. Don't worry, they'll find some way to patch it up. Meantime, sir, I am to tell you that Mr. W. W. Meriman paid for your room and left this envelope for you." The clerk smiled, troubled. "Mr. W. W. Meriman said in case you thought room rent and fifty dollars in spending money was a bribe, he was disappointed in your price—and anyway, he expected you to repay every penny."

Longarm nodded, yawning. "I'm too damn beat to argue. All I want is a bath and—"

"Oh, I'm sorry, Mr. Long. I mean, we got four of the finest hotels here in Silver City, but not one of us is equipped yet with indoor bath facilities. I'm sorry. But we do have eight barbershops downtown, and every one of them offers hot baths." The clerk grinned and leaned across the desk. "A couple of baths have lady attendants. For five dollars, the ladies will wash up as far as possible, and down as far as possible." He went off into peals of laughter. "And for five dollars extra, Mr. Long—now get this, for five dollars extra they'll wash possible."

Longarm smiled tiredly. "I'd laugh," he said, "but I'm so tired I'm afraid my face will crack. Just point me toward the nearest hot bath where a man can wash himself."

"Yes, sir, Mr. Long. Right next door. Granby's Barbershop. Nice hot baths. Fancy new tubs. Fifty cents."

As Longarm thanked him and turned away, the clerk said, "Oh, Mr. Long, there's a young man waiting for you over there by that palm. He asked me to be sure and tell you, the minute you came in."

Longarm turned, and the man leaped up from the club chair beside the straggly palm. He came scurrying across the room, short, thin-shanked, blond-headed. He looked like a shoe clerk except for the notched-handled gun he wore holstered high on his hip under his tweed jacket.

The fellow grinned hesitantly at Longarm, his voice meek. "You Mr. Long? The federal marshal?"

"That's right. What can I do for you?"

"Oh." The man smiled hesitantly again. "I was thinking more what *I* could do for *you*. I been waiting for you. I got a message for you."

"Fine, let's have it."

Troubled, the blond man shook his head and looked around nervously. "Not here, Mr. Long. It's too public."

From long association with mild-looking characters who turned out to have weasel hearts and ferret minds, Longarm tensed. He felt faint hackles prickle across the nape of his neck. He managed to hide a yawn and smiled. "Who'd you say you were?"

That apologetic smile creased the sallow face, and the youth winced. "Oh, I'm sorry, Mr. Long. That's real unpolite of me. Maw always taught me. Be polite, Maw always said."

"Always tip your hat to a man before you shoot him in the back, huh?"

The thin face flushed red, and the mild blue eyes crackled with insane inner fires. "Just a minute, Mr. Long. I never shot a man in the back in my life. My name's J. Z. Banning. You ask anybody about J. Z. Banning. I ain't no backshooter." His laugh was high-pitched. "I ain't no Henry McCarthy."

"Who?"

"Billy the Kid. Kid Antrim. His real name's Henry McCarthy. He used to live here in this town with his maw. After his paw was killed. You know that?"

"I'd heard it."

"You reckon he'll be coming back to town here?"

"I don't know." Longarm yawned again.

"I thought maybe that was why you were here."

"No. I'm not looking for Billy the Kid."

"Thought you might be. He's got hisself quite a reputation, ain't he? Lots of those notches on Henry's gun are for men he shot in the back. At least I never shot nobody in the back." J. Z. Banning sighed, disappointed. "Sure hoped you might have some word on Henry. I'm waiting here for him. I want to be here when Billy comes back to this town. Yes, sir, more than anything in the world, I want to be here."

"I hope you make it," Longarm said without interest.

"Oh, I'll make it. Don't you worry about that. You ask anybody about J. Z. Banning. J. Z. Banning don't back down to no man. J. Z. Banning's the fastest gun alive. You ask anybody."

"I just don't care, son. Sounds to me like you been reading too many Wild West stories. Billy the Kid, Billy Bonney, Billy Antrim, Kid Antrim, now Henry McCarthy. I suspicion half the sawed-off punks in this part of the country are calling themselves Billy the Kid, and the rest are out gunning for him. I reckon the *real* Billy the Kid, whoever the hell he might be, hasn't done anywhere near the stuff that's been laid to him. Take my advice, son, and let it go. Now, what's this message you got for me?"

The boy's mouth jerked nervously, and his eyes darted about the lobby. "Not here. Why don't we just step out the back door to the alley, where it ain't so public?"

"Make it fast," Longarm said. "I'm dead for sleep."

The blond boy smiled oddly. "Oh, I won't keep you long. Won't take long." He turned and started toward the rear exit of the hotel lobby.

Longarm hesitated, then followed. He could see through this kid like tissue paper—another young mustang out to make a name for himself. Waiting for Billy the Kid. He could see the fantasy buzzing in that empty blond head. J. Z. Banning, the gunman who shot down Billy the Kid. Meantime, while he waited, he picked up a few extra bucks in Silver City—from whom? Rancher or miner?

There was no sense in delaying it. If he put him off, he could see J. Z. Banning skittering around, ratlike, in the dark, no matter how much he boasted that he never backshot a man. He was not only sick in the head, he was likely the fastest liar in the West.

"Oh, Marshal!" A voice from the front doorway of the hotel lobby stopped him. "Mr. Long. Just a minute."

He stopped, aware that J. Z. Banning had halted too and was staring over his shoulder, face flushed and contorted. Jesus, the kid's head was like a cave full of flustered bats.

Judge McLoomis and the teenaged boy named Binky Waters came hurrying across the lobby.

Longarm gave J. Z. Banning a faint, taunting smile. "Sorry, old son," he said. "Afraid your date with destiny will just have to wait."

But J. Z. Banning had evidently recognized Judge Lynch McLoomis too. He heeled about and scurried for the back door, going through it and letting it slam behind him.

"Mr. Long, my apologies," McLoomis said.

"I went right straight to the judge's house, Mr. Long," Binky Waters said. "Just like you tole me."

"By the time we got to the sheriff's office, you were gone. And when we got to the marshal's office"—the judge had to hold back an amused grin—"we found the confusion you left behind you there. They had to get a hacksaw to cut the chain. They never could find the key to the iron door. What'd you do with it?"

Longarm shrugged. "I threw it up on the roof of the jail. I didn't mean for them to get out easy. I wanted this town to know what an egg-sucking hound they got for a marshal. I wanted folks to know he got himself locked in his own cell."

"The whole town knows," McLoomis said, trying to hide his smile.

"And the whole town's a-laughin'," Binky Waters said. "We're sorry we didn't git there in time to help you, Mr. Long."

Longarm patted the youth's skinny shoulder. "It's all right, Binky." He faced McLoomis. "I just wanted you to identify me, Judge, in case things got sticky. But I made it all right. Even got back my wallet."

"My God, Longarm, things are even worse than I believed."

"That Marshal Tuttle is a living mess."

McLoomis exhaled. "He always has been, Mr. Long. But that office of town marshal has an evil history. The position of chief town marshal has changed hands nine times in two years."

"If people are smart, Tuttle and his hired guns will be the next to go."

"Mostly the marshals were fired when auditors found shortages in their funds."

"Well, I can guarantee you, Herm Tuttle is on the take."

"Unfortunately, we know that's true. But there's not much we can do about it."

"Don't you know who owns him?"

McLoomis winced slightly. "I don't, Mr. Long. Not for sure. He's done a few things that have fooled me."

"You mean he's for hire to the highest bidder?"

"I'm afraid so. You see, we have special problems here. A town that sprang from a mining boom, stayed alive when other strike sites became ghost towns, and then grew too fast. Why, Silver City was incorporated in 1870—yet it already has the look of a stable old town. But it isn't stable, and it isn't old, and it's still wild. Why, by 1872 there were over three hundred claims had been filed on silver strikes in the area. It was the center of a boom few places have ever known. A lot of the strikes have petered out, but the area's still rich, and there have been a lot of changes. Ranching and farming. And now the laborers and townspeople have built their very own railroad over the Mogollon Mountains—the Silver City, Deming, and Pacific Line. It hauls millions in ore, freight, cattle, food, and lumber. And an even bigger business—that nobody in this world expected—and that's international trade! The collector of customs at El Paso has supervision of New Mexico Territory, but he had to appoint special mounted inspectors for Silver City. Nobody ever dreamed that trade with Chihuahua and Sonora, Mexico, would amount to almost a million dollars a year that had to clear through the Silver City office. And then leading local merchants had to start carrying stocks of value from one hundred thousand up over three hundred thousand just to take care of this international trade for southwestern New Mexico and southeastern Arizona Territory. It all passes through Silver City. That's why the streets are so crowded, and that's one reason why we got this trouble on our hands. Untold millions of dollars pass through Silver City every day, and where there's too much money, men get greedy."

Longarm yawned helplessly. "Yes, sir, Judge, you said it. You got troubles. Right here in Silver City."

Longarm returned from Granby's Barbershop as the sun was turning the sky red and blue and green at sunset. He got his key at the desk, told the clerk to let no one disturb him before nine o'clock the next morning, and stalked up the stairs to the second floor, sagging with fatigue.

His room was large, and with windows opening on Main Street and on Market at the corner, a stiff breeze whipped the curtains and cooled the room.

The bed was comfortable, and he sagged into it. He lay at an angle across it so his feet didn't hang over the end of the mattress. Beds were usually made for shorter people than himself. Noises battered up at him from both streets. And the boom of hard-rock blasting didn't cease when the sun went down.

The mountains and hills echoed with the dynamiting. He was too tired to care. He wrapped a pillow over his head and was asleep in less than five minutes.

An insistent rapping at his Market Street window awakened him. Scowling, he lay for some moments, telling himself it was a bad dream. He didn't know what time it was, but Main Street was as alive in the night as it ever was at noon.

The rapping was repeated. He eased up from the mattress and padded across to the window. It opened on a courtesy roof over the veranda. At first he saw nothing, but then he glimpsed a dark figure pressed hard against the shadowed wall.

"Señor, please," a girl's thickly accented voice caught at him like kitten claws.

"Who is it?"

"It's Katy Codina, Señor. Please . . . I need to talk with you. I not know you were in bed."

"That's where I sleep best."

"Please, may I come in?"

"This is probably going to surprise you, but they have doors in buildings now. And stairs. All kinds of modern conveniences."

"I didn't want nobody should see me come to your room, Señor."

"Great. So you do acrobatics out here on the roof."

"I move very quiet, like a cat in the dark, Señor. I think nobody have seen me yet. I hide real good in the shadows."

She slithered over the sill and stepped into the room with feline grace. By the light from surrounding saloons and pool halls and late-hour barbershops, he recognized the Mexican girl who'd encountered the boar earlier today—or was it two tired centuries ago?

"What are you doing here?" he said.

"Wanted to thank you. To say *gracias*."

"You said *gracias*."

"That was not a proper appreciation, Señor. And after I first see you to my great happiness and relief and safety for my life, I find you are a *federales* marshal, no?"

"I'm a *federales* marshal, yes. And you want a little favor, eh?"

"It is not for me, Señor, but for my poor father. Name of

67

Desdardes Codina, Señor. A good man. From a good family. We have been of these parts it makes many years. Many generations of Desdardes and Codinas. The land we owned was originally a Spanish land grant—from King Ferdinand himself."

Longarm felt his pulse quicken. He'd been sent here because of the land-stealing. He motioned her to a chair. "Sit down," he said, "and tell me about it. You need a light on?"

"I can see very well in this half dark, Señor. The dark makes good for me."

"Well, it makes good for me too, in my longjohns." Longarm sat down on the side of the bed. He nodded toward the only chair in the room. "Go ahead, sit down."

"*Sí*," Katy said. But she sat beside him on the bed. "I think if I am closer—where I can see your face—I can talk better, no?"

"All right. I'll try to remind myself that this is an official visit."

She exhaled heavily. "Oh no, Señor Long. It is no more an official visit than you wish to make it. I am not the kind of *capota* who comes stealing to a *caballero*'s room at night to visit in his—how you say, longjohns?—and pretend official."

Longarm grinned. "So you're not a tease?"

Katy laughed. "When Katy tease, Señor, she not teasing. Eh?"

"Good. So I think if you're going to talk about Spanish land grants, you better start talking fast."

She smiled. "Do not worry. If you get *incómodo*, I make you feel better."

"You're making me uncomfortable, just promising to comfort me. What happened to Desdardes Codina's land grant?"

"The county commissioner, he condemned my father's land and take it from him."

"He can't do that. There's a treaty that says that land is yours in perpetuity."

"But he have taken it. And then he sell it to big corporation."

"You know what corporation?"

"I do not know this. My father, Desdardes Codina, he could tell you better than I—"

68

"I don't know why I'm not saying he should have come in your place."

She smiled. "Perhaps you will be kind enough to talk to him?"

"I purely will. If you'll tell me where your father's place is—what is it, a ranch, a farm?—I'll go to see him tomorrow."

"It is right now neither very much farm or *rancho*. It is what is left when they get through taking the water from him."

"His water?" The words erupted from Longarm's lips. He was so stunned at the brazenness of the theft that he forgot the hardening at his fly. "They can't do that! That's expressly forbidden in the treaty with Mexico—water rights and land surrounding water are untouchable."

"*Sin embargo,* they are gone. If you think you can help my poor father—"

"I know I can help him. All we've got to do is find the crooks who have cheated him, and pluck their tail feathers."

"I shall lead you to the *casa* of Desdares Codina tomorrow, at the hour convenient to you."

"Oh no. This land thing is touchy. Somebody thinks they can start pushing the Mexicans off their land and take their water rights. So far as I know, nobody knows I give a damn about that little land steal, and I want to keep it that way as long as I can. You shouldn't be seen with me. Nobody ought to know you are here."

"I leave quiet. I can move very quiet when I want to."

He felt a slight chill of disappointment. She was indeed a hot-looking little Mexican dish. He had thought he was exhausted, but somehow he hadn't sensed a tired bone in his body since Katy had come through his window.

"All right," he said, "I'll do what I can. That's a promise."

She smiled and wiggled her kittenish bottom on the mattress. "But that is *mañana,* eh, Señor?"

"You have one hell of a way with words," he told her.

Her luminous black eyes glowed in the vague half-light from the street, warm and full of promise. She moved closer to him on the bed.

"I have promise I would be most generous in thanking you for the saving of my life."

69

He started to protest, but decided against it. What the hell, she *did* want to thank him, didn't she? A man had to be polite and accept a gift when it was offered to him, especially in a package like this, for hell's sake.

"Wait until you see what I have for you," she said.

She stood up. She was wearing a dark peasant dress, its color blending well into the shadows. It was low at the bodice, caught at her slender waist, and spilled out about her feet. In a single lithe movement she reached down, caught the hem of the skirt, and pulled it up over her head.

She tossed the dress behind her and stood revealed in total and unabashed nakedness.

Longarm felt his throat tighten, his heart began slugging at his ribcage. This little Mexican was loaded, every inch of her body smooth and gleaming, from rich black hair to the fragile arch of her pretty instep. She was slender, but with hips that were amply rounded, and high-standing, full breasts with small brown nipples. Her flat stomach descended to a dark mound that took his breath away.

She stood in the dim light and let him enjoy the smooth, creamy beauty. "Don't you wish to touch me?" she whispered at last.

"I want to touch you," he admitted. "But I'm damned if I know where to begin. This is almost like too much of a good thing."

"I am most happy that my *caballero* is pleased." She stepped closer and placed her hands on his shoulders. "Would you like me to take off from you the—how you say—*juanlargo?*"

"Longjohns?"

"Sí."

"I'm willing to chance it."

Her slender, shapely fingers moved on the buttons, and the knit-cotton longjohns were seductively peeled away. When he'd stepped out of the underclothes, she reached down and caught him in both her hands, excitedly caressing and fondling him.

He caught her head in both of his hands and turned her face up to kiss. She parted her mouth and he pushed his tongue between her teeth. The way she nursed it threatened to uproot his loins, and he writhed against her. With his lips on hers, he

70

turned and sank back on the bed, with her on top.

She writhed against him in a way that parted her legs and placed her astride him on the mattress. She kept her mouth locked on his, as she undulated her shapely, fiery little hips, raising herself so the throbbing head of his staff was pulsing against the wet heat of her vagina. She came down slowly, encasing him, and he bit his lip hard against the agonizing ecstasy of what she was doing to him. Almost as if she were keeping time with an unheard *zarabanda,* she rocked and whipped upon him, slowly, slowly, and then faster and faster.

Her head thrown back, black hair spilling almost to her driving hips, the line of her throat sharp against the yellow darkness, she impaled herself upon him. Her fingers grasped the cordlike muscles of his shoulders. He began to thrust upward against her, and her nails tightened on his chest. It was the only way she could keep from being bucked across the room.

She moaned, in a muted wailing that got gradually louder. Longarm reached up and caught the nape of her neck in one hand, dragging her down and kissing her to keep her from screaming aloud. With his other hand he caressed her hard-nippled breasts. He was being too rough, and he knew it, but he also knew he couldn't help it. Everything he did was in reaction to her own wildness.

Her lips were locked to his; her tongue lapped at his mouth and chin and mustache, frantically. She had pounded herself down so hard upon him that he was all the way in her, full and deep.

He thrust upward harder and harder and she pressed downward upon him, whimpering in painful delight. Suddenly he felt a shudder wrack through her body, from her toes upward, again and again, in violent waves. She chewed at his mouth, sobbing for breath and saying words he'd never heard before, but in his spinning mind they had a beautiful ring. Suddenly she fell forward upon him, still pressed against him, but totally limp.

"Oh," she gasped, "it was *so* good. Never have I do something that is so good."

He was panting so hard he could barely speak. "You're some fiery little fox yourself," he whispered.

71

"Oh, but—for the first time—I have been drive from my mind. Before, I know what is going on. I scream and wiggle and pretend a lot. I never have nothing like this before."

She pulled away from him reluctantly, and lay with her fragrant hair on the softness of his inner shoulder. "I'm in such a mess," she whispered. "Such a bad mess."

"What's the matter?" he managed to ask, though he was too exhausted to care.

She giggled. "Oh. I come here to thank you for the saving of my life. Now I am more in your debt. Now I have to thank *you*—for doing to me this great things."

"It's all right," he muttered. "I understand."

"But I must thank you," she whispered, her breath hot against his bare flesh. "I do it all. You have to do *nada* but to lie still—and let me thank you."

He would never know if he would have protested, fallen asleep with her caressing his crotch, or fallen in with her renewed fun and games. A sudden, muted knock sounded at his door.

Both of them sat up. In the darkness, Longarm grinned because the naked little Katy Codina covered her bared breasts with her arms.

"What do you know," Longarm whispered. "Somebody's actually using the doorway."

She leapt as lightly as a cat from the mattress. She bent down and gathered up her dress, writhing into it in what seemed one long, fluid action. "It all right," she whispered as the rap sounded again, this time more insistently. "I go out the way I came. I have no wish to—how you say—embarrass you."

She kissed him with a sudden fierceness and padded, catlike, across the room. One moment she was in the shadows beside the wind-blown curtains, the next she was gone. Longarm felt a brief, hard stab of regret.

He got up slowly, removing his Colt from its accustomed place under his pillow. He grinned tauntingly at himself as he grabbed up his longjohns and held them wadded in front of his thighs.

The knock sounded again, louder this time, sharper, more demanding.

"All right," Longarm growled savagely toward the door. "I'm coming."

He crossed the room in his bare feet, feeling the kiss of the night breeze crossing from Market to Main through his room.

His hand on the key, he said, "Who is it?"

"Open the door, Mr. Long," a feminine voice said. "Don't keep me standing out here any longer than you have to."

Scowling, he opened the door a crack and peered out.

The figure outside was shrouded in a black cloak modeled on a monk's hooded cape. It was pulled over her head and wrapped tightly about her body. But he recognized her. He could not believe it was she, but he recognized her. It was Fernanda Maria Louisa Carlotta Salazar, the aloof and regal Spanish *dama* who'd alternately ignored him and kicked him all the way from Socorro to Silver City.

"My God," he said, "what do you want?"

"Hurry. I can't stand out here."

He grinned at her wolfishly. "Well, ordinarily I'd ask you to stay, Miss Salazar, but I'm afraid all I have are leftovers."

Chapter 6

"You can't come in here, ma'am." Longarm moved to close the door. "I ain't dressed."

"Then put some clothes on," Fernanda Salazar hissed imperiously. She was obviously accustomed to giving orders and having them obeyed instantly. Her slender hand struck the door facing with unsuspected strength. The door was ripped from Longarm's negligent grasp and flung against the wall.

Fernanda stepped quickly inside. She spoke along her patrician nose and across her shoulder. "Close that door. At once. Do you want everybody in town to know I'm here?"

Clutching the longjohns against his privates, he closed the door. He said, "I suppose you wouldn't want a lamp on?"

"Certainly not. I can see as much of you as I wish. More, really."

He shrugged again. "You insisted on coming in."

"Oh, you're quite pretty, Mr. Long. For a gringo."

75

He exhaled and went to the bed. He took up the sheet that he and Katy Codina had tumbled and rumpled and twisted on the mattress. He wrapped it, towel-like, about his hips.

"There now," she said in a taunting voice. "You look quite respectable."

"I'm *not* respectable," he growled over his shoulder; this *dama* brought out the worst in his temperament. The hell with her. "I'm not used to parading around naked in front of strange women."

"I'm not a strange woman, Mr. Long. No, I'm quite ordinary, really."

Now he laughed. "If you're an ordinary woman, then the Grand Canyon is an arroyo."

"How nice," she said. "That makes a very pleasant simile."

She unhooked the black silk cape she wore and held it out to him. He took it, the silken fabric whispering against his fingers. Class. That was what this girl had, by the gallon.

Holding the silk cape, he looked about helplessly, and finally draped it negligently over the back of the chair. She laughed at him. "You could have just tossed it in a heap on that bed," she said.

His head came up. "I could have thrown it on the floor."

She gazed at him, faintly amused and at the same time impressed by the width of his shoulders, the muscles writhing in brown cords across his chest, biceps, and ribcage. She said in a half-teasing, half-pleading tone, "Don't be mad with me, Mr. Long. I want to be your friend—or, more honestly, because I want to be honest with you—"

"Oh, please do."

"—I want *you* to be *my* friend."

He exhaled heavily, peering at her in the faint darkness. She wore a wasp-waisted dress of pleated percale. A band of white lace dipped downward from her throat to the deep cleavage at her bodice. The wide hem in the skirt, which was probably four yards around, barely tipped at the toes of her hand-tooled slippers. Her hair was brushed upward from her forehead and neck, a soft black crown about her incredibly fragile face.

Longarm grinned tautly. "I reckon we started out with you kicking the wrong foot," he said.

"I was trying to impress you," she said.

"Oh, you impressed hell out of me."

"I was punctuating W. W. Meriman's sentences for him. His lies. I wanted you to see how many lies that man told."

He grinned and shook his head. "Hell, and I thought you were flirting with me."

"I do not flirt, Mr. Long. When I give, I give completely of myself."

"I'd always heard that Spanish women promenaded and flirted the first half of their lives."

"Perhaps *some* do," she said in a disdainful tone. She sat on the edge of the only chair in the room. She watched him, faint amusement flickering across the sculpted perfection of her features.

Barefoot and wrapped in a sheet, Longarm winced. He understood in that moment a little of how dancing girls must feel in saloons when drunks gawked at them.

"Is being here—this time of night—wise?" he asked.

"In your room? Alone? Are you concerned with my reputation, Mr. Long?"

"Hell no," he said. "I'm worried about mine."

"I assure you, Mr. Long, I came quietly. I parked the coach on a side street. I am accompanied by a most discreet servant coachman. He has been with us since I was a little girl."

"Then I'm sure he's accustomed to your doing just the hell what you want to do."

"That is right, Mr. Long."

"Why?" he said.

"Why? Why am I here?" She laughed faintly. "Don't you know?"

He shook his head. "I'd be a liar if I said I did."

Her voice snagged at him in the wan darkness. "I admire you, Mr. Long."

"You could have fooled me." He walked to the window that overlooked Main Street. The swaybacked avenue was crowded, even at this hour.

"No. You are wrong, Mr. Long." Her muted voice pursued him across the room. "I admire you. I respect you. You are the first gringo—pardon me—the first *norteamericano* for whom I have felt this respect."

"I reckon I'll just have to take that as a compliment."

"You may indeed. My people do not think too highly of your people—boorish, boastful, greedy, swaggering, brawling, insolent, and treacherous."

"Other than that," he teased, "how do you rate us?"

"Very low," she replied seriously. "Even your government is false-hearted and double-dealing. They make treaties to their own advantage, and then rescind them unilaterally when it turns out they were wrong. Surely you heard that W. W. Meriman on the coach. His lies, bald-faced lies! Why, his companies rape and despoil this beautiful land. And for what?"

"Profit," he replied. "Whether we like it or not, Miss Salazar, profit is not a totally dirty word. Profit is what makes the wheels turn."

"Then perhaps the wheels should turn in less destructive ways."

"Have the mines encroached on your property too?" he asked.

He heard her sharp inhalation. She drew herself up rigidly on the chair. "Certainly not, Mr. Long. As big and as ruthless as they are, they would not dare encroach on Salazar land."

"Nobody's tried to condemn any of your land? Or moved to rescind your Spanish land grants?"

She stood up, her hands at her sides. There was almost a pitying look in her gorgeous face. "I see you do not know my father, Mr. Long. A strong, affluent, powerful man, despite his Spanish heritage in a land controlled by bloodless, rootless, immoral gringoes."

"Well, I'm pleased that the New Mexican Territorial Legislature acknowledges your land claims. If there have been no land-jumpers out your way, Señorita Salazar, what's your beef?"

"Beef?"

"Your complaint. You do have complaints—against W. W. Meriman and the other miners? You don't just hate him for lying?"

"A man who lies, Mr. Long, will steal. A man who steals will kill."

"I know, and the next thing we know, he'll stop going to Sunday school altogether. What are your charges—cold, hard facts—against W. W. Meriman and men like him?"

"Oh, we have beefs, Mr. Long. Believe me, we have them. My family more than all others."

"That's what I want to hear," he said.

"Do you? Why?"

"Why are you here, lady? Because I'm a lawman, ma'am. If I am going to help you, I've got to know what your complaint is."

Her lovely mouth twisted into a haughty and petulant smile. "Do you pretend that any lawman—especially a federal lawman—is going to do anything to help anyone but the big-business pirates?"

"Why don't you go on home, it's getting late."

"All right. I'll tell you what they are doing to my lovely country. They are poisoning it. The water, the creeks, the streams, and even the wells. They are ripping out lovely old live oaks that are hundreds of years old—"

"I grant that. They don't give a damn what the country looks like, as long as they make a buck. Like I say, though, it's hard to stop them spoiling the country unless what they are doing is against the law."

"You mean that poisoning water isn't a crime?"

He sighed. "They're trying to make it one, Miss Salazar. You should have spent less time kicking me and more time listening to W. W. Meriman. The Anti–Hydraulic Mining Act would stop a lot of the contamination of drinking water. You heard W. W. Meriman. He's fighting passage of that law with every cent he's got."

"That's why men like him have got to be stopped. Mr. Long, the Salazar lands have been in my family for nine generations. Nine generations. And they are far lovelier, far more beautiful and fertile than it was when King Ferdinand signed the grant. We have husbanded the land, protected it. We have grown our gardens and our fruit and our cattle and horses upon it. We have put back many times more than we have taken from it. That is why I am pleading with you to help us stop the miners and men like W. W. Meriman."

He sighed. "You're right. There's a lot of right on your side. Let's put it this way—in any way that Meriman or the others encroach on your rights, I'll fight alongside your father to stop them."

She stood up, exhaling deeply. "That's what I came to hear."

He grinned. "Why didn't you tell me that's what you wanted? I could have told you that an hour ago and saved all this time. We could both have gotten some sleep."

She walked slowly toward him in the gauzy veil of light, smiling oddly. "Are you certain you are so anxious to sleep, Mr. Long?"

He straightened. "You don't have to do this, Miss Salazar. I am tired, and I have agreed to help you people all I can. Nothing else you can do is going to ensure that I'll remain loyal to you."

She smiled. "Let me be the judge of what will increase your loyalty."

He laughed and shook his head. "Miss Salazar, this could be considered a kind of bribery."

"Then let them indict me," she whispered. "The truth is that you are a beautiful man, Mr. Long. I have been all this time unable to take my eyes off of you. You excite me."

"Wait a minute," he said. "There's something else I've heard about you Spanish *damas*. I've heard that your men consider you women in two ways—angels and sluts. If he can have you without a wedding ring, you are a slut. If he can't, you are placed on the old pedestal."

"That's quite true, Mr. Long. Men are stupid. Nationality doesn't change that, unfortunately. Spanish men are less hypocritical about their views of women than are you *norteamericanos*. The men of your country feel the same way. If they can beat down a woman's defenses with lies, promises, passionate caresses, then she's a slut. If they can't, she is a good woman. Are you such a damn fool, Mr. Long?"

"I should hope not," he answered fervently.

"Undress me then," she said, standing before him with her arms at her sides. "You do want to look at me, don't you?"

"As God is my witness."

He drew her to him and kissed her. He felt her heart pound savagely against his bare chest. With his lips still hard upon hers, he unfastened the row of buttons along her spine and peeled the dress off her shoulders and slipped it down, letting it fall in a dark pool about her feet. He saw that in one way the grandee's daughter and the little washerwoman were alike—they each came to him without any underwear.

"My God," Longarm whispered. "You knew you were going to do this all the time."

She laughed softly. "Does that make me a fallen woman, Mr. Long?"

"Call me Longarm," he whispered against her mouth.

"I like that better," she said.

She slid her hands down his sides, loosened the sheet from his loins, and let it fall to the floor next to her dress. Her fingers traced lightly across his chest, over the flat plane of his belly, to the hardness that stood between them, quivering.

With her lips open and her tongue trailing between them, she drew her mouth along his throat, to his chest, and down. She knelt before him, her arms going about his hips, her long fingers grasping his buttocks. She pressed her face for a long moment into his pubic hair and then moved her mouth along his rigidity, as if measuring it with her lips. Suddenly she grasped it between her teeth and drove herself furiously upon it, nuzzling madly. She drew back only long enough to gasp, "Oh my God, it tastes good!"

"It's a blend," he said. He caught the sides of her head in his hands, massaging his fingers frantically in the richness of her ebony hair. All this time, her hand continued to caress and fondle his testes. She stroked him and bit him and nursed him until he thought everything inside him was going to pour out.

Suddenly she drew away from him. "I've got to have it— in me," she gasped. "It's too wonderful to waste."

He laid her down on the bed and she sprawled there with her black hair spread out over the white sheet, her knees bent and legs spread wide. She reached up and caught his staff, pulling it urgently into her hot wetness.

As if goaded by devils, Longarm drove into her, deep and full. She moaned from deep inside her and locked her ankles around his waist, pressing her hips against his. She caught his head in her hands and pulled his mouth down to hers, chewing at him as he thrust harder and harder.

He felt her respond in whimpering pleasure at each thrust, and he reached into her as she had never been penetrated. She gasped aloud, rocking her head back and forth, but always pressing her mouth upon his. Abrupty, an orgasmic shudder wracked her. He moved faster, feeling himself going out of control, flooding everything he had into her.

She wailed in a muted cry of ecstasy and then lay still. Longarm fell away from her and sagged across the bed. He heard her whispering to him, but he had no idea what she was saying. Whether he wanted it or not, sleep overwhelmed him.

He woke up chilled, lying naked across the bed, and alone. The noise had abated, if only slightly, down on Main Street.

And then he was aware of something else. Someone was knocking at his door. He laughed in tired exasperation. He didn't know any other women in this town. Except Miss Nellie.

Longarm grinned tiredly. He knew better. One thing he'd learned about the nervous Miss Nellie, she wasn't the type to go out looking for it. She didn't have to—she had it delivered.

He turned over in bed, deciding the hell with them, whoever they were.

The rapping was repeated, louder this time. Swearing, he pulled his Colt out from under the pillow for the second time that night, and considered, for one insane moment, the possibility of simply putting a slug through the door. He decided that was likely a violation of some local ordinance, though, so he called out, "All right, relax. I'm coming."

As he padded across the floor, he came more fully awake and realized that he had fallen asleep before Miss Salazar left, and that therefore the door was unlocked. He shook his head. Sloppy, sloppy. He was becoming careless in his dotage.

Flattening himself against the wall next to the door, he called out, "Who is it?"

A quivering voice came through the door's thin wood. "It's Marshal Tuttle, Mr. Long. I sure would appreciate it if I could talk to you."

"Jesus," Longarm said, "what time is it?"

"Just a little after three," Tuttle's reply came back.

"I got nothing in God's world to say to you, Tuttle, at three o'clock in the goddamned morning."

"Please," the man begged. "Just two minutes."

I must be crazy, Longarm thought. He reached out and yanked open the door, and Tuttle stepped into the room, staring about, trying to adjust his eyes to the darkness. Longarm kicked the door shut behind him, and Tuttle started as he turned and found himself gazing down the barrel of Longarm's Colt Model T .44-40.

Longarm reached out and removed Tuttle's revolver from its holster, then walked back across the room and lit the lamp on the bedside table, laying the town marshal's sidearm beside it.

"Two minutes, Tuttle," he said, turning. "I reckon you better say your piece quick."

"I hate to bother you this time of the night—do you always sleep naked like this?"

"Haven't you ever seen a grown man naked before, Tuttle?"

"Well. I mean. Most men I know sleep in nightgowns. I mean, naked—night vapors and all. You could get almost anything."

"I *got* almost everything." Longarm yawned helplessly. "Now what do you want?"

Tuttle watched him drape a rumpled sheet over his shoulders, Indian fashion, and nodded, smiling hesitantly. "I know it's late. But I couldn't sleep. Went to bed before ten tonight. Just laid there. Couldn't sleep. Sweating. Thinking. Rolling from one side to the other. Martha finally got up and went to sleep in one of the kids' rooms. I got something on my mind, Mr. Long, and it's driving me crazy."

"Maybe it's called a conscience, and you just never knew you had one."

"Oh no, it's not that. I've learned to live with my conscience. Yes. Yes. I've had to, you know. A marshal in a town like this—if he lets his conscience get in his way, why, he won't last very long. No. It's bigger than that. It's ruin. I face ruin. And I'm here to beg you to help me."

"I can't think of anybody offhand that I'd rather say no to, Tuttle."

Tuttle's face screwed up as if he tasted the metallic tinge of defeat. He shook his head, gesturing meaninglessly. "I know you have every reason to hate me, Mr. Long. The way I acted and all—"

"I know," Longarm said in a cold, dead tone. "The oldest alibi in the world. You were following orders."

"I was. I was. My God, you know I was. I was told to tell

you to get out of this town and keep going. I knew what they meant. They meant they'd kill you if you hung around."

"You want to tell me who 'they' are?"

Tuttle trembled visibly. He looked as if he might fall. "My God, Mr. Long. Oh my God. If I were to do that, why, I wouldn't live to get home."

"What loss would that be, Tuttle? Who in God's world would give a goddamn if a muddleheaded, sneak-thief like you was squashed?"

"Nobody. Nobody. You're right. Maybe Martha might cry a little. And my youngest daughter—she—she's a little partial to me. But I come about your badge and papers and identification. I knew they were stolen from you. But that's it. I had no part in stealing them—or accepting the stolen goods."

"You didn't mind using them against me, once you got them."

"I was doing—"

"What you were told. That's getting old and stale, Tuttle."

"Believe me, Mr. Long. Your wallet was brought to me earlier today. By a town kid. I can give you his name."

"Don't mind sacrificing the little people, eh, Tuttle?"

"He was just a town kid. He found those things outside a livery stable corral. I swear to you, that's where he found them. He brought them to me. I'm not a crook, Mr. Long. I'm stupid, I admit that. I acted stupid. But I'm not a crook, and I'm not mixed up in whoever held up that stage. I mean, this job is all I got. If I lose it . . . I don't know . . ."

"Where'd the kid say he found the wallet?"

Tuttle winced and nodded. He kept nodding, as if, once he got started, he couldn't stop. "Out on Broadway, Mr. Long. Les Shaw's Livery and Corral. That's where he swore he found it. On the ground outside Les Shaw's corral."

Chapter 7

Longarm walked slowly along Broadway in the early-morning sunlight. Sleepless faces peered at him from red-rimmed eyes; men who had not been to bed last night were bravely facing the new day.

He didn't know what he was looking for. In fact, he doubted his own sanity for even believing Marshal Tuttle. The man was a habitual liar; he had to lie to stay where he was—lie to the city, the world, his family, and himself.

Still, Longarm had wakened early. Though he'd thought he'd sleep until noon, at least, he lay sleepless on the bed, turning over in his mind the things he'd heard last night. Finally he said the hell with it, got up, washed under his armpits and in his crotch, dressed, ate breakfast in the hotel dining room, and headed out, looking for Les Shaw's Livery Stable and Corral.

It was two days now since the robbery. Little chance he'd find any sign around a busy corral.

Les Shaw's Livery Stable and Corral looked like a thriving

business. The big wooden barn had been painted in the past two years, and the stables were clean.

Longarm walked around the barn. In the open ground out back, between the corral and the stable, he prowled aimlessly, knowing that the odds and time were against him.

He found nothing, but he was less than disappointed, because he hadn't really hoped to turn up anything out here. He walked over to the corral, hooked his shoe over a low pole, and rested his arms on the top crossbar, planning his next step. It looked as if a visit to Desdardes Codina was indicated. Why not rent one of these animals for the ride out?

He started to turn away, then his head jerked back. He stared at the milling horses inside the corral, his heart slugging faster. He gazed at the dappled, gray-faced horse.

He wheeled around and strode into the stables. Near the front door a lean, tall youth in Levi's, denim shirt, dung-stained boots, and shabby straw hat sat against a wall, holding a *Police Gazette* in one hand and his pecker in the other.

When he heard Longarm approaching, he jerked his hand away from his fly guiltily and put the pink-papered magazine over his lap. "Yes, sir. What you want? Want to rent a horse?"

"I might. First I want to know if you keep records of horses you've rented."

"Yes, sir, we do. We write the names down. When they take a horse out. When they bring 'em back."

"You've got a dapple-faced gray in the corral out back. I want you to look in your book and tell me who rented the gray two or three days ago."

Reluctantly the youth got to his feet, embarrassed by the bulge at his crotch. "Forget it," Longarm told him. "A cock that size is nothing to be ashamed of."

The boy grinned sheepishly. "It's them ladies in the *Police Gazette*. I mean, they show everything. They even show their garters."

"Lord have mercy," Longarm said.

The boy nodded seriously. "Just like the preacher said in church last Sunday. Don't know what this world is coming to."

The youth opened a ruled ledger. He ran his fingers down the scribbled pages, squinting and reading with his lips. At last he looked up and shook his head. "The dapple-face is ol'

Buster, mister. He ain't been out in the last week."

"The hell he hasn't." Longarm, angered, flashed his badge. "I think you better check again."

The boy nodded. Trembling now, he went over the pages carefully. "No, sir. Nobody. Ol' Buster ain't been out."

"Is your boss around?"

"Not this time of the morning. He gets a hankering for a woman right about breakfast time. He's likely over to Miss Nellie Pyles' Fandango. He's right partial to her girls."

The twenty-four-hour Fandango Saloon was open but quiet before ten in the morning. Four men slouched silently at a poker table. A couple of cowpokes sagged at tables with unfinished mugs of beer. A swamper mopped the floors. Behind the gleaming bar, a bartender polished glasses. None of the ladies was in evidence. The bartender looked up and grinned. Longarm said, "You know whether a man named Les Shaw is around this morning?"

The bartender went on grinning. "Come on now, friend. Even if I knew a thing like that, how long would I keep my job if I told what I knew?"

Calmly, Longarm took out his wallet and flipped it open. The bartender stared at the badge, stopped smiling, and nodded. "He's upstairs, Marshal. In Miss Nellie's suite. I don't think they're going to take kindly to you disturbing them."

"They probably won't."

Longarm walked up the wide stairs, feeling the eyes of the bartender fixed on his back. He went along the silent, cavernous upstairs hall and knocked on the third door.

At first nothing happened. By the time he was getting ready to rap the third time, the door was yanked open and Miss Nellie turned the air blue with expletives.

Her eyes widened as she recognized Longarm. "Well, Mr. Long, you got the urge fast, didn't you?"

"I got the urge the first time I looked at you, Miss Nellie."

"Well, look, could you come back—this afternoon? I am kinda tied up right now."

"Tied up, eh?" he said. "Is that the kind of thing that cleans ol' Les Shaw's shovel?"

Miss Nellie wore a feather-collared, diaphanous wrap-around, high-heeled slippers, and nothing else. She stared at Longarm. Behind her, a man's voice called, "What gives, Nellie? I'm catching pneumonia."

Miss Nellie spoke over her shoulder. "Just a minute, Les." She faced Longarm again. "Now just what do you want?"

"I want to come in and talk."

"I told you, I'm busy."

"It's Mr. Shaw I want to talk to."

"Well, I don't think Mr. Shaw wants to talk to *you* right now."

"Well, if this was a friendly call, Miss Nellie, I'd take no for an answer. But I'm here official, and I want to talk to him. Now. I don't much give a damn what *he* wants."

Miss Nellie smiled wanly and stepped back. Her transparent robe spilled open along the front, revealing a shapely, highly powdered body with the red marks of Les Shaw's fingers on it in strategic places. She ignored the garment, watching Longarm's face oddly.

Longarm entered the frilly, curtained, mirrored room. A large four-poster bed with cupids carved on it dominated the white, woolly carpeting and vanity dressers. Huge closets spilled Miss Nellie's gowns, dresses, shoes, lingerie, and hats. Cloying perfumes and colognes were almost overpowering in the suite.

"What the hell is this?" the man on the bed said. Longarm couldn't say why, but he was shocked at the appearance of the naked man. He'd expected someone older. This fellow was in his twenties, with the over-handsome features, body, and arrogance of a theatrical leading man. He was well built, muscular. He smiled in a cold, wolfish way. "We trying something different this morning, Miss Nellie?"

The madam shrugged. "Nothing new about a *ménage à trois,* Les. This is a federal marshal. He wants to talk to you."

Buck-naked, Les Shaw swung off the bed and strolled over to Longarm, hand extended, completely unselfconscious. "Good to meet you, sir. What's your problem—besides being impolite as hell, barging in on a man at a moment like this?"

"I saw a horse over in your corral," Longarm said.

"Hell, you see something you like, buy him. Or rent him. Talk to Hank."

"I talked to Hank. He told me that ol' Buster hasn't been out of your corral in the past week."

Les shrugged. "Then that must be right. We keep records on those rental nags. Now, I admit, once and a while, things are kind of casual. A man cuts his own horse out of the corral, saddles it, returns it, and pays for it. Long as he pays for it, we ain't too particular."

"Somebody took that horse out—two, three days ago," Longarm persisted.

Les shrugged again. "If it ain't on the record, Long, I know nothing about it."

"Nobody's told you my name."

Shaw grinned. "Hell, man. Nobody has to tell me your name. Everybody in this town knows a U. S. marshal named Custis Long is in Silver City, pushing people around—locking the town marshal in his own cell."

Angered, Longarm said, "I could arrange one of those cells for you too."

Shaw's bland expression did not alter. "Now, Marshal, why would you want to do a thing like that?"

"To improve your memory. I'm warning you. I will throw your butt in jail, and you won't get pussy before breakfast. I want some answers from you, Shaw. Straight answers."

"Hell, what do you want to know?"

"Who took that horse from your corral. Ol' Buster was the horse used in the stage holdup. I memorized that animal because it was all I had to go on. And Marshal Tuttle told me my wallet was found outside your corral."

"Who can believe Herm Tuttle?" Les Shaw yawned and sat on the side of the bed. "You put me in jail, Long, and I'll get your ass for false arrest. I've done nothing. I've answered your stupid-ass questions. If that's all you've got to say, get the hell out of here."

Longarm stared down at the handsome man. "That's not all I have to say. If there's no record of anyone renting ol' Buster, maybe you took him."

"Me?" Les Shaw put his head back laughing. "Come on, Marshal."

"You mind telling me where you were, day before yesterday afternoon."

Les grinned rakishly up at him. "Can you narrow that down?"

Longarm considered this a moment, then gave the stableowner a precise hour. Les Shaw grinned crookedly. "Sure, I can tell you where I was at one o'clock day before yesterday afternoon." His smile taunted Longarm. "Only I don't think I ought to, old son."

"Well, I think you better, *old son*, if you want to stay out of jail."

"Now, Long, I don't like to compromise a lady's good name."

Miss Nellie crossed the room. She said, "He was with me. Right here. On this bed, Marshal."

"Jesus," Longarm said. "Don't you do anything but stud work?"

"Sometimes." Les Shaw shrugged. "So, my sex drive is kinda strong. Is that a crime?"

"There's a crime here somewhere," Longarm said. "But I think it's covered up in powder and perfume."

"Why, Marshal, would you accuse Miss Nellie Pyles of lying?"

Nellie had fired up a match and lit a cigarette, and now she took a deep drag on it, exhaling smoke through her nostrils. "Les is not lying, Marshal. And I'm not lying. Les likes his sex some on the weird side." She casually exposed her breast, livid with his hand prints. "He says beating a girl until her tail is fiery red and hot is the only way to warm her up. He's a little too rough for most of my girls—stuff he wants, they can't handle like I can."

"Old-fashioned sex gets old fast," Les said. "I like variations. I think 'em up. I run over here and Miss Nellie and me try 'em out."

Longarm's mouth twisted. "What you're saying, old son, whether you know it or not, is that you don't like women at all. In fact, you hate 'em. You have to beat on 'em to get your jollies."

"You sound like one of those prudish sex books, Marshal. My preferences are none of your business. And unless they are a federal crime, you can get the hell out of here, because whether you approve of my sex life or not, I was right here, day before yesterday afternoon, right between Miss Nellie's sweet-smelling thighs."

Longarm decided to hell with Les Shaw's corral. He wouldn't even rent a horse from the pretty bastard. On the street outside Miss Nellie Pyles' Fandango, he asked a man for directions to the nearest livery stable. The fellow looked up from the shaded table where he and another oldster played tiddlywinks. "That would be Tom Cook's place, mister. Right over on the next street. Bullard. Can't miss it. Right down there by the Mud Bridge."

Riding a docile gelding with a center-fire saddle, Longarm headed south out of town. He had gone less than a quarter of a mile when he heard the fast-pounding hooves of a racing horse behind him. He pulled up the gelding in the shade of an oak and sat with the flap of his frock coat shoved off his high-holstered cross-draw.

Les Shaw came riding fast, fully dressed, with holstered gun and sheafed rifle on his saddle. He looked handsome astride his horse, and Longarm was sure he knew it.

Shaw pulled up on his horse and reined in beside Longarm, dust smoking across them. "Where you headed, partner?"

"South."

"I'll ride along with you."

"I don't think so."

"Now come on, old son. I'm going to get the idea you don't like me."

"Whether I like you or not has nothing to do with it. I just don't need you."

Les Shaw stopped smiling. "You see? That shows what you know. You're a lawman—and maybe a good one, Long. But you're too trusting. Too damned trusting for your own good. Haven't you realized yet, man? There is a price out on your head, and plenty of rascals around here figuring how to collect."

Longarm remembered J. Z. Banning's inviting him out in the alley behind the Exchange Hotel for a "message." Then there was Deputy Marshal Eastwood Tyne's threat. And he reckoned there were hotheads who would pay to have him erased before they found out whether or not he was a threat to their particular little shell game. He shrugged. "It's always open season on feds," he said.

"But this is killing time in Grant County, old son, and you're the clay pigeon. What the hell? One of my horses caused you a bad time. Let me ride along with you and make it up. My being along improves your odds by that much."

Longarm shrugged and heeled his mount, heading down the trail south out of Silver City.

They followed the trace at a steady pace, not hurrying, but not lagging either. Low-hanging clouds scraped their bellies on the jagged crests of tall and distant blue hills. They rode silently for the most part. Once, Shaw said, "You want to say where you're headed?"

"No." Longarm shook his head and they fell silent again. The country changed often and amazingly, from pine groves to oak-tufted knolls to flats so dry that even the cactus didn't grow anywhere except in gray creekbeds.

Few other people passed them on the stage road. The stamping mills and smelting furnaces and most of the mines were in the mountains north and west of the town. They passed a few Mexican farms, but mostly this was wild, isolated country.

They started up an incline that wound through a rocky pass across overhanging foothills. Shaw's horse lagged slightly, probably winded from the hard ride out to meet Longarm.

It grew quieter as they climbed. A strange, taut silence pervaded the metallically sunlit day. No animal stirred in the thickets, no bird screeched in the trees. Faintly troubled, Longarm straightened in his saddle, listening.

He tilted his head and caught the whisper of sound above and behind them, in the rocks to their left. The sound was almost nothing, a loosened pebble clattering on the hard ground.

He turned and caught the glint of sunlight off a gun barrel on the rock ledge.

He did three things in the same movement, from old habit. He yanked his horse hard to the left against the boulders beside the trace, then drew his gun and slid from his saddle.

He turned toward Shaw. "Duck," he said. "Move."

As he spoke, the rifle was fired from the ledge above him.

Les, his gun already in his hand, was leaping from his saddle, and this was all that saved his pretty hide.

The bullet struck him, all right. Longarm heard the dull splat of lead in flesh. He waited only to see Les, white-faced and grimacing with pain, spin and fall against the rocks at the side of the roadway.

Longarm was already clambering upward between the rocks, toward the place where he'd seen the glint of sunlight on the gun barrel.

He stayed low, running at a half-crouch in the protection of the boulders. He kept waiting for the second shot, but it didn't come.

Cautious, he slowed, climbing upward stealthily through the rocks, his finger taut on the trigger of his Colt.

He reached the place where he'd seen the gun, and found the ejected shell casing. It was army issue. He heard the sound of a small avalanche below him.

Pressed against the boulder, holding the hot casing, he watched two coyote-thin Apaches, bare-chested, in Indian-agency-issued Levi's and moccasins, each carrying an army Springfield rifle, running pell-mell toward two mustangs ground-tied in mesquite clumps at the foot of the hill. As he watched, the Indians leaped on their ponies. They rode away fast, not even looking back. He stayed where he was for a moment, watching them raise dust clouds, before he returned down the steep incline to the road.

Les Shaw had not moved from where he'd sprawled against the rocks beside the road. He was gray. He gripped his right arm with his left. His gun lay on the ground beside his leg. "Goddamn, it hurts," he said between gritted teeth.

"Thought pain made things interesting," Longarm taunted him.

He knelt beside the youthful hostler. Longarm's quick, cursory glance told him that the wound was superficial. The rifle slug had ripped through the fleshy part of Shaw's upper arm, at the shoulder. "If it didn't hit bone," he told Shaw, "it shouldn't be too bad. Won't worry me at all."

"You son of a bitch," Shaw said between clenched teeth.

"Beginning to recover, are you?" Longarm bent over the man and ripped away his shirtsleeve. He probed at the bloodied shoulder. "Bullet went right through," he said. He punched at the muscles and Shaw gasped in pain. "You should take more exercise. You're getting flabby."

"Oh, you're a smartass son of a bitch, aren't you?"

"You're the one who wanted to follow me out here. Now shut up and let me check it. If I had some water, I could wash it out, and you'd live to flog women another day."

"Water in my canteen, on my saddle," Les said. He winced with a sudden stab of pain. "You get a look at the bastards?"

"Couple of feisty Indian kids. Didn't look to be more than fifteen."

"A fifteen-year-old can still kill you dead," Les said.

Longarm knelt beside Shaw and washed the wound. "You better head back to town," he said. "See a doctor. Except for being stiff for a while, it ought to heal up good. Hell, you're lucky, you could have been shot in your tallywhacker."

Les Shaw drew a deep breath. He took up his gun and thrust it back into his holster as if he hated the weapon almost as much as he hated himself. "I would have been killed," he said, "if you hadn't yelled. You saved my life."

Longarm shrugged. "What the hell."

"Plenty." Shaw shifted his weight against the rock, his face twisted. "When you turned, I had my gun out—ready to back-shoot you."

"Yeah. I figured that. Not right at first. But by the time I got back from up there."

"There's a hell of a price out on you. I figured I could use it."

"You could still have gotten me as I came back down through those rocks."

"No." Shaw grinned tautly. "You were moving pretty smoothly. Thinking. Anyhow, you'd saved my life. And killing you after that wasn't all that easy."

"You don't mean to tell me that hearing the flapping of angel wings has given you a touch of that old-time religion?" Longarm taunted.

"Go to hell. I thought I could kill you. I couldn't. Not even for all that money."

"You want to tell me who paid you to shoot me?"

"I don't owe you *that* much, old son." Les drew a long,

painful breath and held it. "It wouldn't buy you anything to know. You either got to get out of town, or stay on guard. You got *no* friends in Silver City. I don't care who smiles at your face, you got *no* friends."

Longarm sighed and then shrugged. "What the hell, I never came here to be voted Queen of the May."

Les Shaw stared at him, his face gray. "Don't you understand what I'm trying to tell you? I owe you that much, and I'm telling you straight. They're going to get you. Today, out here. Or tonight, or tomorrow."

Whatever else Shaw might have intended to say was lost in the rasping crossfire of rifles above them. Bullets splatted into the road or smashed against boulders. Longarm hit the ground and wriggled into the rocks above the road. After a moment he heard Shaw wriggling painfully after him.

Longarm pressed in close against the rocks, searching above them. He hadn't seen any muzzle flash, but the sounds of gunfire came from both sides of the road. Somebody was trying to pin them down in the pass. Up to this moment they'd done a pretty fair job of it.

"Those goddamn Apaches," Les said, panting. "They must have doubled back."

"Those kids were scared shitless," Longarm said. "They're running yet. Whoever it is, it's not those Indian kids."

They heard movement in the rocks, a showering of pebbles on the shale. "It's white men," Longarm said, and added in contempt, "clumsy white killers."

Holding his breath, Les crawled around the boulder to the road. Longarm heard him whispering to his horse, trying to coax him near. Maybe he was going to make a run for it. He didn't blame him.

A few moments later, Les returned, pulling the animals as far as he could into the narrow opening between the boulders. "I'm good with animals," he said. He removed his rifle from its saddle scabbard and tossed it to Longarm. "I can't use it, winged like this. Be my guest."

Longarm nodded. He watched Les remove a pair of field glasses from a cowhide case tied to his saddlehorn. Shaw crawled back among the rocks and put his back against a boulder. He remained with his eyes shut and his teeth clenched for a long beat. Then he said, "Stick your hat up there on the end of the rifle."

Longarm took off his hat, placed it on the rifle barrel, and worked it slowly against the rock facing, as if he were climbing carefully into the open.

A rifle cracked from across the road. The bullet smashed into the rock mere inches from the hat. Longarm jerked it back.

"Those bastards don't give a damn for the price of hats," he said. But Shaw didn't answer. He held the field glasses pressed against his eyes, watching the place where the rifle fire had come from.

In a moment, panting, Shaw lowered the glasses and grinned coldly. "I got the one across the road. A hired gun. New to town. Working as deputy marshal."

"What else?" Longarm said.

"His name is Hawes," Shaw said. "Beak Hawes. Ugly son of a bitch, too. You want to put your hat up on this side of the boulder, we'll get a look at his partner."

Longarm gingerly raised the hat on the end of the rifle barrel, then jerked it back quickly and raised it again. He heard Shaw's admiring laugh. "That's good. He's craning his neck like an egret up there, trying to get a bead. It's Tyne. Ole Eastwood Tyne."

"I met him."

"You locked him in his own hoosegow, with his boss. It's real personal with Tyne. You made people think he's no smarter than Tuttle. He's never going to forgive you for that."

Longarm looked around and found a greasewood stick. He placed his hat on the end of it. "Run it up there," he said. "And I'll take a shot at Mr. Tyne."

But before they could change places, shots came from a new angle, from behind them. They hit the ground and crawled forward. "They've moved on us," Shaw said.

"Sons of bitches mean business."

Chapter 8

Lying prone and pressed down hard, as if trying to hide behind a pebble, Longarm chewed thoughtfully on the edge of his mustache. Aloud, he muttered, "I can't understand it. I just ain't worth all that money."

Shaw spoke from close beside him. "In Silver City you are, old son. Lot of money in that town. A man wants something done right, he's willing to pay the freight."

Longarm said, "I've been thinking about you fellows trying to knock me off—for pay. Killers like Tyne and Hawes are expensive. I don't know what the town fathers of Silver City are up to, but they sure as hell don't want anybody nosing around."

"You got it." Shaw pressed closer to the boulder as the rifles chattered away again. "We got a good thing in Silver City. A real good thing. It's a wide-open town. A wide-open country. The biggest profit to the toughest, smartest hombre. Plenty of gravy. Now me, I'm not greedy. I don't give a shit about being a millionaire, I just want to live like one. Business is good at the livery stable. I want to be sure it stays that way. Only way to be sure that happens is to be sure the mines stay open, and the big cattlemen get what they want, and international trade keeps pouring through like a funnel. I'm just like the rest of the boys, I don't want any of that to change."

"And you think I'll change it?"

"You'll sure as hell try. It's your job, and one thing I know about you by now. Unless somebody kills you off, you're going to do your job—for your fucking two hundred a month—"

"One hundred a month and expenses."

"Jesus. That's even worse."

Gunfire cracked again above them, closer this time, the bullets digging into the dirt around them.

"Time to move again," Shaw said, writhing forward around the boulder.

Longarm followed, but snarled, "This crawling shit is getting tedious."

"Wait a minute," Shaw said. "I got a better idea." He laughed coldly. "Maybe we can both get out of here—if not together, at least alive."

"I'm listening."

"They know we're both down here. They also know that Les Shaw is not against making a few dishonest bucks, but he *is* against working with the law. You crawl forward as far as you can. Poke your hat up on a stick or something where they can see it. While they're pinning you down, I'll fire my gun and you fire yours. Then I'll get on my horse and ride out of here. They'll see me winged. They'll jump up to check on me—I hope—before they start shooting. Maybe they'll think I've shot you."

Longarm grinned coldly. "Maybe I'll think so too."

Shaw grinned. "It's my way of repaying you, old son. First payment. Last payment. If I can get you out of here alive, we're square. I owe you nothing, you owe me nothing."

Longarm shrugged. "I'll chance it."

Pushing his hat on the greasewood stick above and ahead of him, he wriggled low between the rocks. The gunmen went wild above him, and bullets whistled and screamed past him.

"Now," Shaw said from behind him. He fired, and a bullet whistled past, inches from Longarm's head.

Longarm flung himself over. "You son of a bitch," he said. He shot at a stick near Shaw's shoulder. Shaw yelled in fear.

"All right, you law-enforcin' bastard," Shaw said. "We're quits. See you in hell, old son."

There was silence in the rocks above them. It was clear that Tyne and Hawes were trying to figure out what had happened between them.

Suddenly, long before Longarm thought he could make it, Shaw had swung up into his saddle and was racing away, his right arm hanging like a broken wing, toward Silver City.

On his knees, the rifle hard against his shoulder, Longarm watched the rocks above. He saw Tyne leap to his feet. Automatically, Longarm pressed the trigger. Tyne went leaping away, out of sight.

Holding his breath, Longarm waited. The silence stewed and boiled over and ran down through the rocks from up there. Then, suddenly, he heard horses' hooves on the roadway.

Leaping up, gun ready, he ran from between the rocks. Beak Hawes was on the lead horse, grasping the reins of the other. Tyne was wavering in the saddle of the second mount, and would have fallen except that he was tied down.

Kneeling, Longarm took aim at Hawes's broad back and pressed the trigger. The gunman was too far away. The crack of the rifle only speeded him up.

The *casa* of Desdardes Codina was adobe and cedar, with shake-shingle roofing. It sat under the meager shade of a single cottonwood tree in fields burned crisp and crackling dry. Nothing seemed to grow on the place but bare-assed kids, slat-sided cows, flat-bellied burros, and willow poles strung with baling wire to hold washing.

The smaller children came running when they spotted Longarm approaching. Older boys and girls came out of the shade, watching, arms shading the sun from their eyes. One of the children opened the gate for Longarm. He grinned and thanked them. "Your father around?" he said.

They stared at him blankly. He spoke haltingly. *"Es esto el rancho de Desdardes Codina?"*

"Desdardes Codina! Desdardes Codina!" they screamed, jumping up and down.

An older boy, about twelve, in hand-me-down tweed pants and denim shirt open to the belly button, came forward. "I am Esteban Codina, son of Desdardes Codina. I speak some of the *Inglés*. Can I help you? *Qué desea Usted?"*

Longarm smiled and nodded. *"Yo deseo hablar con su papá, Desdardes Codina."*

"You wish to speak to my father?"

"Right. I couldn't have said it better. Tell him it is Marshal Custis Long from Denver."

The children started chanting his name. "Coos-tees Long! Coos-tees Long!"

As if he'd been listening behind the door, which stood ajar, Desdardes Codina came running from the house. He was followed by a stout but still pretty Mexican woman who once may have looked like her daughter Katy.

As if the hot sands burned his feet, Desdardes Codina ran out with his hand extended. *"Mi hija,* Katy, have say that you are coming to see me. She is saying that if help there is, you will make it. May God bless you, Señor, *y bienvenido a mi casa."*

Longarm swung down from the saddle. Two of the small boys grabbed the reins. "I wonder if I could have some water for my horse and me?" Longarm said.

He saw the glance exchanged between Codina and his wife. But Codina nodded and the whole squadron trooped around the shack to the area where clothes flapped in the breeze on the baling-wire lines, and chickens clucked fiercely, outdone only by the screeching of guinea hens.

The children led his horse to a pool of faintly green water. The horse sniffed and snuffed at the greenish liquid, but refused to drink it.

Meanwhile, Codina had dipped a gourd of water from the rock-enclosed, ground-level well. Grinning, he handed it to Longarm.

Longarm took a sip. The water had a metallic taste, but he

100

forced himself to swallow it, no longer thirsty. He nodded, thanking Codina, who took the gourd and emptied it back in the well. "We don't dare to waste one drop of water, Señor."

"It looks pretty dry," Longarm agreed.

"There is water," Codina said. "But the mines in the hills above us, they are *emponzoña los arroyos*—they poison the streams." Codina led the troop to inspect the cows, which barely stood, and had little interest in grazing. In fact, they looked damned near dead.

"We get no milk these days," Codina said. He led the way to the garden. "This is the work of Violante, *mi esposo, y nuestros niños*. Once the garden was green and grew well."

"We ate good from our garden," Esteban said, as if quoting something.

Codina nodded. "But no more. Since the water is *despojo*—espoil by *las minas*— we don't eat too good."

Longarm winced, looking around. "Looks like you've got nothing but *niños* and troubles, Señor Codina. And—" He pointed toward the small gray puffs of smoke rising from the encircling hills. "Apache smoke signals."

Codina smiled and shrugged. "*Los indios*. She don't bother us, Meester Long. We do not bother them. They let us alone also."

"I heard some chief had taken the Apaches off the San Carlos reservation."

"*Sí. Es verdad*. The great chief of the Apache since the Mexican army kill Victorio is Geronimo. He have been named chief after Cochise. But the braves around here are under Chato—*el jefe* of the Chiricahua Apache, and under Huavichi, a renegade chief."

"I hear there have been killings."

"The Apache go his way, hunting. He makes the trouble only when hungry. He comes close in to town then. Not long ago, Loco and some Warm Springs Apache steal horses to eat—from corrals near Silver City."

"But you are not afraid?"

Codina gave him a strange smile. "Of the *indios?* No, Señor, no. When they come to our gate, it is because they have empty bellies and want food. We try to feed them as much as we can.

They can see we have very little. Sometimes they bring us *un conejo* or a small deer."

"The *norteamericanos* are calling for help because of the Apache raids," Longarm said.

"These raids come, I theenk, when the Apache is hungry. *Los norteamericanos* run in houses when Apache come. Board windows. Lock doors, start shooting. They kill an Apache—" Codina shrugged. "Then the Indians burn them out."

"It's a hell of a problem."

"*Sí. Es muy malo.* But I think it will be settled soon. When all Apache are dead, then it is settled." Codina gave him a sad little smile. "I think that not be too long. There is no clean water for the Indian to drink. No animals for him to feed on. And if they camp, the army massacres their women and children. It not be too long for the Apache, I theenk."

Longarm shook his head and exhaled heavily. Sometimes he was able to tell himself he represented the greatest nation on earth, but at other times he felt sickly, as if he represented the very forces of absolute corrupt power and injustice. He said, "And what about you?"

Codina gave him a wan smile. "I theenk maybe it not be too long for Codina too. No?"

"I don't know, Codina. We'll see what we can do. Where is this land that has been taken from you?"

Longarm stood, rage moiling deep in his belly, and stared at the barbed wire strung at a long angle across the greenest, highest area above the Codina hut. Every hundred feet was a neatly lettered sign: *"Property of Houston-Grant Land Company. Keep off. Trespassers Will Be Shot."*

Codina swung his arm. "All this land, she was mine. In my family many generations. A land grant from King Ferdinand of Spain. On it are the natural springs. *Mira,* among these trees you will see—how you say?—artesian well."

"I can smell it," Longarm said.

"*Sí.* Smells *muy malo.* But it is very good water. Clean. From very deep in the earth. It makes my garden very green— once."

"They just took your land where there was water?"

"*Es verdad,* Meester Long. All where the dry *arroyos* are

102

that are little rivers in the wet season, they are gone and forbidden to me. Yonder, there is one creek from high in the mountains. Maybe from the crest of the Divide, you know? Seldom is it dry. We could once tell storms in the high ranges that we could not even see, by the rush of flooding in this creek. She too is lost to me now."

"Jesus. Didn't you complain?"

"Complain, Señor? Where does an hombre like me go to complain? My friend Ricardo Martinez, he complain to the mine about dumping their slag on his land. They smile in his face, and yet somebody keel him on his way home. And many others. Not alone *mejicanos*. Gringos too dare not complain."

"How do they go about taking land away from you?"

"They condemn it, Señor."

"For what reason?"

"They do not bother to say. They say it is the law, and if I got the money, I can fight it. I got no two *pesos* to rub their faces together. They come first, Meester Long, with the offer to buy. Even to a poor man, the money they offer for lands with springs and creeks, she is insult. So you say no. Then, either they kill—as they killed Maricas Del Rio, Sanderson Smith, and many others—or they condemn. So I nod my head. And so I live with this condemn, if you are calling this living. I reckon I must thank God that I am left alive—for a while at least—with Violante and my cheeldren. No?"

Longarm sighed. "I don't want to give you any hope, Mr. Codina. Hell, I don't know what I can do. But this—" He pulled at the barbed wire, then released it so it sang crisply in the silence. "It's all against the law."

Codina stared at him. "I try to tell *mis niños* this when they cry from the empty belly tonight, Señor."

Longarm rode back into Silver City, the rage building inside him. He had wondered if Codina could suggest a new way back into town, since he had no doubt that killers lurked along the stage road. Codina had smiled. "Esteban will take you on the trail we use—we come in on other side of town."

The sun was a dry yellow ball in a cloudless sky at midafternoon. He was thankful there was time to start checking on the land grabs. Otherwise it would have churned in his belly and stuck in his craw all night. These thieving sons of bitches had to be stopped.

When his horse plodded into town on Market Street, he felt a tide of tension racing ahead of him like a wave lapping up high on some sodden shore. People's heads jerked up. They stared at him as if they'd never expected to see him again. He saw one man heel around and run across vacant lots toward Hudson Street.

Longarm watched the toadies scurry. Let the rats run. Let them spread the word that Longarm was alive and well and in Silver City to stay. They could dig him out by the roots, and that was the only way. There was one other way, but he knew in advance that it was an option these vultures would never consider. They could obey the law. . . .

The balding man behind the high desk in the tax office was giving Longarm a hard time. As soon as Longarm had told him what he wanted, the man's face flushed and he began shaking his head. "You're out of line, sir, coming in here and making demands of me."

"Am I?" Longarm gazed innocently at the sign on the door he'd purposely left open on the County Building corridor. Aloud, he read the wording on the door facing: "'Tom Houghton. Property Appraiser. Tax Collector. Homestead Information. Land Titles.'" Longarm laughed ironically. "All under one tent, eh?" He looked about the busy office, at the clerks at their pinewood desks, the filing cabinets, the plat books, the tax records, the American flag. "Easier to handle if there ain't too many palms to be greased, eh?"

"I don't know what you're talking about, sir."

"Well, I'm going to tell you. You are Tom Houghton, aren't you? 'Appraiser. Collector. Homesteads and Titles.'"

"I am Tom Houghton, sir, and I am a busy man."

"You sure as hell are, Tom. You boys have been running around breaking more federal laws than a three-handed pickpocket."

Work stopped in the room. Clerks looked up from beneath green eyeshades. Pens ceased their scratching, and even breathing was suspended.

"Why don't you close that hall door, sir?" Tom Houghton said.

Longarm shook his head. "Let's leave it open, Tom. I need the fresh air."

"You'll have to keep your voice down if you expect me to talk with you at all, sir."

"Why? You mean you think these people in this town don't know how crooked this office is?"

"I don't know what you're talking about," Houghton said, "but I advise you to keep your voice down and get out of here."

"No. Not until you tell me what I came in here to find out."

Houghton laughed nastily and shook his head. One thing about him: Longarm had never seen a bureaucrat more secure in his niche, whatever it was. "I'm not hired to make people like you happy, sir."

Longarm shrugged. "I don't want happy, Tommy. I want honest. I want justice. I want compliance with federal statutes."

"I've heard enough. Get out of here. Now. Or I'll send for the law."

"Sorry, fella. You're too late. I *am* the law."

Tom Houghton leaned across the high desk, his piercing gaze fixed on Longarm. "Just what is it you want, sir?"

Longarm grinned at him coolly. "Well, let's start off easy, Tom, old son. Why don't you give me the names of the people who are principal owners of the Houston-Grant Land Company?"

Houghton's bland smile matched Longarm's. "I'm afraid I can't do that."

"And how about the Border Land Company?"

"I can't give you that information either."

"And also, while you're at it, I want the names of the principal holders of the Arizona-Santa Fe Land Company."

"Is that all?"

"That's all for a start."

Houghton moved to turn away. "Then I'll bid you a pleasant good afternoon, sir."

"You walk away from me, you son of a bitch," Longarm said flatly, "you're going to come crawling back."

Houghton heeled around. "Why don't you get out of here?"

Longarm slapped his open wallet, with badge and identification, on the tabletop. Houghton took his time reading it, then he looked up and shrugged. "You'll have to show me more than that, Mr. Long."

Longarm's mouth twisted sourly. "How much?"

Houghton's face went pale. "You're arrogant and insulting. I don't have to take this kind of abuse."

"No. All you've got to do is hand over the information I want."

"When you show me a subpoena, Mr. Long, I'll discuss the matter with you. Until then, I advise you to get out of my office."

Longarm stared at the pale, taut face and smiled mildly. "A subpoena? Is that all you want, Tommy? Hell, why didn't you say so? You got it."

He turned, walked out, and slammed the door so hard that it rattled on its hinges.

Judge Lynch McLoomis got up from behind his cluttered desk in his office on the second floor of the County Building. He came around it, smiling. "You look like you've been eating chili and tacos, Mr. Long."

"Just about. My stomach is upset, all right. I just met Tom Houghton."

McLoomis sighed. "Tom can do that to you, all right. You see, Mr. Long, Tom is more than a *member* of the court house gang. He knows where the bodies are buried. All the bodies. He's a bastard. But I'd say he's the most secure and well-fixed bastard in Grant County. Dynamite wouldn't blast him out of his job."

"I want a subpoena. I want the names of the principal owners of Houston-Grant Land Company, Border Land Company, and Arizona-Santa Fe Land Company. He says he'll turn it over when I bring a subpoena."

Judge McLoomis looked ill. He went back around his desk and sat down in his high-backed chair. He studied the backs of his hands.

Longarm's voice rasped. "Don't tell me you're going to get coy on me?"

McLoomis winced and looked up, shaking his head. "Not

at all. I'll sign a subpoena right now. But it won't do you any good. It's just part of the runaround you're going to get, Mr. Long. Tom's down there right now, laughing at you. He knows you'll get a subpoena. But you'll find, when you take it to him, that it can't be served on him, or the county commissioners either. It must be served on the Speaker of the New Mexico Territorial Legislature, when that body is in session—at Santa Fe."

"What kind of law is that?"

McLoomis leaned forward and lowered his voice. "It's one of the protective laws these people have pushed through the legislature. It's self-perpetuating. It's self-protecting. It's almost ironclad."

Longarm paced the room. He stood at the window, looking down at the midafternoon action on west Broadway. Over his shoulder, he said, "I want to know who runs Houston-Grant. And by God, I *will* know."

McLoomis said, "We better keep our voices down, Mr. Long. The walls in this building have ears. Sometimes I think they have eyes."

Longarm walked back to the desk, his voice muted. "You're telling me it can't be done? I can't fight 'em and win? Even with the U. S. government behind me? I don't believe that, Judge."

McLoomis peered at him across the desk. "So that's why you are here. The land grabbers violating the Treaty of Guadalupe Hidalgo."

"That's right. The law that states that Spanish land grants are to be held in perpetuity—unless sold by the original family's heirs."

McLoomis smiled oddly. "My God. I've wondered if there were men in this state so powerful that the United States government was going to keep its hands off this criminal land theft."

"Nope. I've been sent here to end it, and I will. They can stop me one way. They can kill me."

"Don't think they won't try."

"They've already tried. They'll try again. But that's why I know the people I'm dealing with are stupid. They haven't even sense enough to see that if they kill me, the U. S. Department of Justice will just keep sending marshals."

McLoomis drew a deep breath, then let it out. He glanced around his office and then lowered his voice again. "I may be able to help you."

"I'll take any help I can get. You get me just a pry, and by God I'll rip open holes with it."

McLoomis nodded. "A man named Jacob Catron."

"What about him?"

Judge McLoomis nodded. "Jacob Catron had Tom Houghton's job. But Jacob had one thing that Tom never developed— a conscience. When the evil got cancerous, Catron got sick at his belly of the stench. He came to me and wanted to swear out warrants against the people who were killing, stealing, condemning land, and passing laws to make their activities legal in this territory."

"What happened?"

"He left my office and somebody shot him. They didn't kill him, but—"

"They discouraged the hell out of him."

"That's right. As soon as he could travel, he went to live in Lordsburg. That's about fifty miles from here. A new town, founded last year, when the tracks of the Southern Pacific went through on the old Butterfield stage route. It's a railroad shop town now. Jacob lives there—paralyzed in one side—with his family."

"I'll go see him."

"No." McLoomis lowered his voice even more. "That would never do. If you got to Lordsburg alive, you and Jacob would be sitting ducks on the way back."

"What makes you think he'll come back?"

"I know Jacob. He loves this beautiful country as much as I do. What these people are doing to it sickens him. He can give you the names of the Houston-Grant people and the others—but I better warn you, you may be in for a shock."

"No. I've met the good people of Silver City. It would take a hell of a lot to shock me now."

"There are decent people in this town, Mr. Long. Maybe they just need to be reminded that they *are* decent people."

Longarm shrugged. "If you say so. How do we go about getting Catron or his deposition?"

McLoomis lowered his voice another octave. "I can bring him. Or I can get his deposition, sworn and attested to in Lordsburg."

"You think these rats won't kill you?"

"No. My wife and son and I go to Lordsburg several times a year—every holiday. Mrs. McLoomis's family lives there now, and we visit them. I'll have my wife pass the word around the sewing club that we're going on a short vacation down to Lordsburg. Honoria is as good as any woman in town at spreading the word. That way, no one will suspect a thing."

Chapter 9

Longarm strode along Main Street in the late-afternoon heat. Shadows fell long across the washed-out ditch of a thorough-fare, and the westering sun probed among crannies between faded buildings. A piano tinkled with incongruous gaiety in the Bedrock Saloon. People stared at Longarm, some with open malice in their faces, but none of them spoke to him.

When he reached the Western Union office next door to the Fandango Saloon, he saw Miss Nellie Pyles, decked out in a frilly, fresh-looking, lime-green dress and feather boa. She rocked in the shade near the end of her porch—away from the swinging doors, where traffic was heaviest—and smoked and drummed her fingers.

Miss Nellie smiled and waved when she spied Longarm on the walk. He touched his hatbrim to her politely, but entered the telegraph office. He stood at the desk and composed a telegram to Governor Wallace that was going to fry Billy Vail's eyes when he got the bill. He explained that carefully planned laws prevented his learning names crucial to his investigation. He named the companies—Houston-Grant, Arizona-Santa Fe, and Border Land—and asked that the territorial governor demand that these names be revealed to him, by return telegraph if possible.

The telegraph clerk counted the words, whistled faintly, and told him the message would cost almost a dollar. Longarm shrugged. "Hell, it may even be worth it," he said.

As he turned away, the clerk said, "Oh, Mr. Long. We've got messages from a Mr. Vail in Denver for you, and a money order for one hundred dollars, payable to you."

Longarm thanked him and took the money and messages. He stuffed the telegrams in his frock coat pocket, too full of rage to read any threats from the chief marshal. The money he placed in his wallet.

He paused on the stoop outside the Western Union office. Miss Nellie's voice raked at him like kitten claws from her porch. "No hard feelings, Longarm?" she called from her rocking chair.

He grinned tautly. "Not yet, ma'am."

She laughed with him. "You are a devil, Longarm. I didn't mean that. I mean I hope you are not mad with me because Les Shaw and I gave you a bad time this morning."

"Bad time?" He shook his head. "What bad time? Anything that happens to me in this town, I figure as ordinary, run-of-the-mill ill will."

"Why, Longarm, what a terrible way to talk," she said. "Some of the nicest people in this world live right here in Silver City."

"If they do, they haven't come out from under their rocks, because I sure as hell haven't seen them."

"Why, look at me, Longarm, you don't know how nice I could be."

"Yes I do. You and Shaw gave me some idea this morning."

"Why, Longarm, you're just depressed. You come right over here. We'll go on up to my suite and have a few drinks and get you back your sweet disposition."

He smiled, but shook his head. "Les Shaw is one act I could never follow, ma'am."

She laughed. "Les is walking around with his arm in a sling. He won't be spanking any of my girls for a few days. Not right-handed, anyway..." She lowered her voice. "By the way, Longarm, you were right about Les Shaw."

Longarm stared at the madam, his heart beating faster, hopeful. Maybe somebody would tell him the truth. Maybe he'd get one break, anyhow. "Oh?" He tried to keep his voice casual, not wanting to scare her off if she was going to talk about the stagecoach holdup. "Was I?"

"Yes, you were. Les does have to be violent to get any thrill at all from sex. I think it's because he was always such a beautiful boy—a handsome young man. Every woman tried to spoil him. He had so much sex thrown at him that he got fed up with the ordinary kind. It takes a lot of variety to excite him."

"Oh." Longarm sighed heavily. "Is that right?"

Longarm whistled incredulously at his first sight of W. W. Meriman's office in the Revolutionary Mining Company Building. The male secretary had ushered him into a room the size of a public assembly hall, with huge windows that overlooked the mountains above town.

Meriman got up from a vast, polished desk and high-backed green leather chair, angled so it commanded a view of the hills through those windows. He grinned. "I got whatever I have from those hills. When I feel low, I can stare at 'em and remember—and thank God I'm sittin' in here."

He laughed and shook hands with Longarm, inviting him to sit in a deep, overstuffed club chair. There were no ordinary chairs in Meriman's office. Even those lined along his gleaming conference table were padded and covered and glowing with the sheen of affluence. Longarm had never been in such an office, and he doubted that many others had, either.

"Lordy," he said. "There's nothing like this in Denver."

"Denver?" Meriman laughed. "Where's Denver?"

Even with the conference table and the bar along the inner wall, there was space and breathing room, and the Persian carpeting seemed ankle deep.

Meriman offered Longarm a cigar, and when he lighted up,

he was afraid he'd be ill from such mellow flavor, after those two-for-a-nickel cheroots he chewed on. "Good God," he said. "This could be habit-forming."

Meriman grinned, shrugged, and flopped in one of the deep club chairs facing Longarm. The marshal dug money from his pocket and counted it out on the desk, which reflected each greenback as he set it down.

"Much as all this costs," Longarm said, "I figure I best repay you fast."

Meriman shrugged. "Just tried to help you out a little, Long. Damned little. You and me are likely going to end up in a deadly struggle, so I reckon you payin' me back makes us about quits."

Longarm sighed. "Wish it could be different. You're one hell of a character. Never met anybody like you. Wish it could be different."

"Well, it can't be. I'm a miner, smelter, shipper, handler, prospector, and speculator in silver, Long. Silver is my life. Hell, silver ain't the only metal in these hills. Why, the first gold strike around here was right over at Santo Domingo gulch. The hills are rotten with copper. It's just that silver is my life. And silver mining. And nobody—not the President, not the goddamn United States government—is going to tell me how to run my business. I *know* how to run my business. I learned the hard way. By doing it.

"And I'm not the only silver miner." He grinned. "Just happen to be the biggest and the richest and the orneriest, that's all. Hell, I wasn't even the one that hit the first strike around here. Bullard and his people did that, at the Legal Tender mine. It's just that I hit the biggest strike the world had ever known up to that time. I started the rush of people here. I was here at the beginning.

"I don't tell you that to brag. I don't mind boastin' a bit, but I'm telling you because I want you to know I've put my blood and guts and sweat and heart in this thing, and I ain't about to lose it, and I ain't about to bend to the will of a bunch of addle-headed politicians in Washington, D.C., or up in Santa Fe. They think to stop me with Anti-Hydraulic Mining Acts. Fuck 'em. They can pass acts till hell freezes over, but I'm going on mining the way I have to to get metal out of this rock.

114

"Hell, that ain't easy. It's not placer mining or panning, like out in California or up Nevada way, or even in Montana. Minerals are not easy to get at. They're all what is called smelting, or refractory ores, and they have to be assayed by fire. Jesus, when I was young and broke and hungry, I near ate my burros waiting weeks after a strike before I could just learn its value!

"And bad as that was, that wasn't our biggest problem. Hell, we had nothing *but* big problems. Our mining was most handicapped by the simple, stupid lack of tools and the money to buy tools. And hell, you couldn't buy steel for drills, gads, and hammers at any price!

"But we persisted, and blasted and picked the stuff out, and stamped and smelted—and we shipped unrefined silver. Hell, my biggest mine kept *nine* adobe smelters running around the clock, milling ore that they *embezzled* from *my* mines.

"And getting the ore to market! Sevens months by ox and mule trains, run by Mexicans who didn't give a shit in this world about time! Seven months to the nearest railhead and back. Hell, the muleskinners used to plant corn and potatoes and plant gardens at their campsites every night. Then they'd stop and harvest the stuff on the return trip! Ore had to be rich. We threw valuable silver in the dumps just because it cost too much to refine and ship it!

"I realize you don't give a damn, Longarm, but I want you to see my side of it. I'm in business. I'm in business to stay. You can hack that in stone and send it off to Denver or to Washington or to God in heaven."

Longarm regarded the miner through a haze of sweet-smelling blue cigar smoke. It was hard to hate a man who smoked such expensive tobacco.

"All right. That's your side. Now you want to hear mine?"

"Nothing I want to hear more, old son."

"You people are getting laws passed that outrage the common sense of ordinary people."

"Like you?"

"I came in today, all around Robin Hood's barn, to keep from getting shot by somebody's hired guns on the south stage road. I came in from a Mexican farmer's place that is being wiped off the face of the earth—his water poisoned, his cattle

115

dying, his gardens ruined, his children sick—because you silver people dump the drainage of your mines and smelters into washes and creeks that run across the land of these people."

Meriman shrugged. "I'm sorry as hell to hear about your Mexican friend. Sounds like he ought to sell out. Something has got to give, Long. Can't you see that? If we have mines, the water has got to go some danged place, don't it? It's too damned bad that the washes drain poisonous acid waters into springs, wells, and other drinking water down slope. But, like I say, it's got to go somewhere. And we got to have mines, or we can give up and let little Juan raise his kids and his gardens. Shit, Longarm, does that make sense to you?"

"That land is *theirs*."

"Hell, then let them sell, if they're in the way of progress. Silver, that's progress. Who gives a damn in hell if a few skinny scrub cows die? As a matter of fact, who cares if a few skinny scrub *folks* die, if they won't sell out and move?"

"There's nobody to sell out to. Nobody has to buy from them, as long as you people can condemn their lands and water holes, and simply take it from them."

"Hell, I don't know anything about that."

Longarm had opened his mouth to speak, but at the casual sincerity in Meriman's tone, he found it hard to believe the miner was lying. He was laying his cards on the table, but not accepting responsibility for anything that was not his fault.

"Land companies are condemning Spanish land-grant lands," Longarm said. "You mean you miners aren't prospecting illegally on private property—and then condemning to get the lands you want?"

"Somebody might be. I'm not. Longarm, do I have to remind you that the Treaty of 1848, ending the Mexican War, gave the Spanish land-grant people perpetual possession?"

Longarm laughed in spite of himself. "No you don't. That's what I came here to remind *you* of."

Meriman rang for his secretary, and ordered drinks for Longarm and himself. "We'll drink and be merry," he said. "For by tomorrow we may be at each other's throats."

"All you got to do is stop violating the Treaty of Guadalupe Hidalgo," Longarm said, "and you and I got no fight at all. I could wish you were more human toward people downslope from you, but the arresting offense, as far as I'm concerned, is land theft."

"Afraid you're barking up the wrong tree, old son. I'm a business man, that's all. No more. No less. If there's a war—with anybody—we miners are in it to the finish. But we're just fighting for one thing—the right to do business."

"And what about the rights of others—the right to stay alive on their own lands?"

"Longarm, you're shooting blanks at me. If you think I'm stupid enough to violate a federal law about land grants, if you think I'd get mixed up with crooked two-bit politicians in some Santa Fe Ring, I'm sorry for you. You underestimate me.

"And one more thing. If you're down here trying to cripple my business, that's too bad. I wouldn't walk across the street to help you ruin me. But as to *somebody* hiring guns to kill you or anybody else, that's an insult to my intelligence. Just as I am not stupid enough to try to bribe you or any other United States marshal, by the same damned token I'm not stupid enough to pay to have one of you fellows killed for doing your job."

It was almost dark when Longarm walked out of Meriman's elegant office. Shadows crouched in every alley. As the sun set, the hills above the town lost their angularity and sharply defined planes. Darkness settled slowly upward through the ravines, leaving the gaps somber and chill; the forbidding, tall crests were now slashed with fearful dark gorges and bottomless black canyons.

He felt light-headed and slightly giddy. He hadn't eaten since breakfast, and Meriman's tasty liquor had been persuasive. He'd had too much. People seemed to dance little jigs as they passed him on both sides on the flag walks.

Talking with Meriman—or listening to him, rather—had also unsettled hm and left him troubled and dizzy. He was no longer certain of the truth in this Silver City assignment. Meriman had *sounded* truthful. At least, Longarm believed him. He couldn't look at Meriman in that magnificent office up there and believe the man was hiring paid killers to skulk in alleys. If Meriman wanted another man dead, he'd go out and face that hombre with his own gun.

117

What Meriman believed, he acted upon. What Meriman wanted, he tried to take. Meriman didn't break laws, because that was a fool's game. God knew, Longarm agreed with him on that.

Longarm glanced about the quiet yet watchful street. The hell with them. First they tried to kill him, and now they tried to confuse him. The hell with them. Only one thing mattered here. Crimes were being committed, and that shit had to stop.

He'd listen to everybody, but he was damned if he'd be suckered by any of them, even those handing out rich-tasting cigars and smooth whiskey.

He walked in Jesse's Cafe on Bullard Street. The place was crowded with miners and townspeople, but the noise was muted and it grew quieter when he entered.

A waitress showed him a table. He gave her a grin. "What else is good, honey?"

The waitress smiled back at him. "The Silver City Enchilada is good, sir. It was invented right here in town."

"I'll chance it, and some baked potato and black coffee." He watched her walk away, her outline dimmed and slightly out of focus, but pleasing nevertheless.

The Silver City Enchilada, when the waitress served it, was a regular hot enchilada with an egg fried sunny-side-up and placed on top. "Oh my God," Longarm said. "It's watching me."

He ate his dinner, ignoring the covert stares. Gradually the tempo of the conversations picked up again, but the sounds flowed around him and didn't touch him. In fact, he felt isolated in the busy room. The hell with them. He punched the egg in the yolk with his fork and watched the yellow flood down over the enchilada. . . .

The street was completely dark when Longarm came out of the cafe. He let the door close behind him and stood for a moment in the shaft of light through the restaurant window. He felt the rising night breeze down off the snow-capped Mogollon Mountains, refreshing him. The food had sobered him up—hell, that was the trouble with food. It sobered you up every time, and left you with nothing to face but reality.

He glimpsed the movement of shadow inside shadow at a

long angle across the street. He lunged away from the lighted window, drawing his Colt as he moved.

"Hey, Long!" A man's disembodied voice yelled from the dark alley. "Over here."

The man shouted and fired at the same time. Longarm's body was still clearly outlined in the lamplight. Two shots, so close together they sounded as one. Instead of leaping deeper into the shadows, Longarm crabbed to the right. The bullets smashed into the adobe wall of the cafe. Before his assailant could fire again, Longarm was sprinting forward, drawing, running across the street toward the alley.

Longarm crouched low, his Colt in his fist, watching that black-shadowed alley. Behind him and around him there was a confusion of sounds—yelling, the pounding of running feet. He ignored all the noises, everything driven from his mind but the man in those shadows.

At the corner of the alley, the crouched man raised his arm to fire again. This slight movement was all the target Longarm needed.

Still running, Longarm fired twice, aiming low. Unless his bushwhacker was on his belly, he was hit for sure.

A loud wail of pain bellowed out of the darkness of the alley. A barrel was knocked over, and it rolled out a few feet into Bullard Street. Crouched low, Longarm kept advancing. The figure was huge in the shadows, broad and heavy-bellied. Longarm fired again and the yelling stopped. The big man plunged headlong from beside the building wall.

Shouts rose from all directions, and people came running. English mixed and blended with excited Spanish, none of it intelligible.

He could see the fallen man plainly now, in dim lamplight from the street windows. The fellow sprawled prone in the mud of the alley, his arms stretched out in front of him as if he were still trying to crawl forward. His big hands dug into the dirt. His gun was almost a foot from him where he'd flung it in his agony.

Longarm exhaled heavily, standing over the prostrate form. He jerked his head toward one of the babbling onlookers. "You know this man?" he said.

The man stared down at the barely moving form on the

ground. "Oh my God," he said. "Why, that's Deputy Marshal Beak Hawes."

A burro-drawn hay cart was hitched to a post at the curb. Longarm asked who owned it. A Mexican came forward, nodding his head, his hat in his hands.

"Oh my God, I'm dying," Hawes gasped. Blood leaked from the corner of his mouth.

"Hell, that was what you wanted, wasn't it?" Longarm asked, as he lifted Hawes and threw him into the bed of the hay cart. The Mexican clambered up on the seat beside Longarm. "You wish to take Señor Hawes to the hospital?"

"Hell no," Longarm said. "They might be able to save the son of a bitch. Take us to the jail."

Hawes wept and cursed from the bed of the cart. "God Almightly. God Almighty. I'm in pain, man. Get me to a doctor."

Longarm glanced over his shoulder, but said nothing.

"God damn you," Hawes wept. "You merciless bastard, you. If I had my gun, I'd kill you."

"You had your gun, Hawes, and look where it got you." Longarm glanced at the Mexican and said conversationally, "Some hombres never learn, eh?"

The Mexican stared at Longarm, but said nothing. The minds and actions of the gringos were far beyond his ken. He shrugged and slapped the reins, trying to hurry the burro.

When the cart pulled up before the marshal's office and jail on Hudson Street, the Mexican bobbed his head. "You wish I to help you get Señor Hawes inside?"

"Naw. You've done enough." Longarm swung down from the cart. He tossed the Mexican four bits. The dark man bobbed his head.

Longarm walked around the cart, caught the big deputy by the coat collar, and yanked.

"Jesus," Hawes gasped. "You're killing me."

Beak Hawes's huge body landed hard in the street, with the sound of a dropped watermelon.

Still clutching the deputy's collar in his left hand, Longarm dragged the man across the walk and up to the stoop of the building. The Mexican sat gape-mouthed, watching.

Longarm drew his gun and kicked the front door open. When he stepped inside, Tuttle and three of his deputies were on their feet, guns drawn.

Holding his own gun before him, Longarm ignored the weapons in the hands of the town marshals. He dragged Hawes into the brightly lighted office and almost to Tuttle's rolltop desk. The men lowered their guns, staring in shock at Hawes, bleeding and writhing like a fish out of water on the floor.

Tuttle stared at Hawes, then brought his gaze up to Longarm's coldly raging face, shaking his head. Tuttle looked sick at his stomach. He laid his own gun on his desk and spread his hands impotently.

Longarm caught the glances of contempt exchanged among the young deputies as they watched the ineffectual marshal. They didn't even pretend that Tuttle was their boss in anything but name. These gunslingers were hired not by Tuttle at all, but by Tuttle's bosses, whoever in hell they might turn out to be.

"What—what in hell have you done?" Tuttle whispered, his face agonized.

"Doctor . . . get me a doctor," Hawes pleaded.

Tuttle nodded toward one of the deputies, who holstered his gun, moved toward the front door, and then stopped, watching Longarm. When Longarm shrugged his wide shoulders, the deputy ran through the front door and into the street.

Tuttle came from his desk and knelt beside Hawes. He stared up at Longarm. "My God! You've got poor Tyne in the hospital, not expected to live. And now Hawes."

"Your man Hawes, decent law-enforcement officer that he is, tried to bushwhack me from an alley over on Bullard Street, Tuttle. I'm sure you'll find witnesses to what happened. Whether you do or not, the bastard tried this morning to kill me out on the trail. He tried again tonight. Only this time the fat bastard's luck ran out."

Hawes moaned deep in his barrel chest, and rolled on the floor, choking on his blood.

"The doctor's coming, Beak," Tuttle said. He straightened and gazed at Longarm. "Are you planning to kill us all, Long?"

Longarm shrugged. "Not unless I have to. You see, Tuttle,

121

bringing Hawes over here to you was just part of it. I came to give you a message. Hear me, Tuttle, and hear me clear. You're next."

"What?" Tuttle shook his head and retreated two steps. "What? What? What?"

Again, Longarm intercepted the glances of contempt for the town marshal that passed among his deputies. "Now just a minute, Long. What in hell are you saying?" Tuttle's fat hands trembled.

"I think you heard me," Longarm said in that calm and deadly cold voice. "The next one of your so-called deputies that takes a shot at me, Tuttle, I'm coming to get you."

"Oh my God."

"So think on it, you fat, crooked bastard," Longarm said. "One more attempt on me, and I'm coming to get *you*, Tuttle— with my gun in my hand."

A sob wracked Tuttle's rotund body. He backed up a step, then retreated to his desk, where he stared up at Longarm, shaking his head helplessly.

"Oh my God," Tuttle whispered. He sat in his swivel chair. It squealed dryly under his weight. He looked around, shaking his head. "What will I do?"

"That's up to you, Tuttle," Longarm said. He holstered his gun, glanced toward the two deputies, turned, and walked out.

Chapter 10

The moon cleared the horizon, bright and yellow, and Main Street was dark and loud, as Longarm walked back to the Exchange Hotel. He had a lot of puzzling things buzzing around in his mind, but was too tired to deal with any of them. Somewhere a clock tolled nine times. Longarm yawned helplessly, exhausted.

The swaybacked Main Street was busier at this hour than it had been at midmorning. In the hills, the hardrock men worked by lamplight, setting their dynamite and blasting out their ores.

When Longarm entered the lobby of the hotel, the night clerk spoke his name and motioned to him from behind the desk. But Longarm shook his head and kept walking. Whatever the crisis, he was too tired to deal with it. He was going to keep his door locked tonight against all intruders, male or female. And even if Katy Codina tried to come in, by God, he'd lock his windows. He yawned again, shaking his head, as he went up the stairs two at a time.

When he came off the stairwell at the second floor, he saw his door standing open and light spilling into the wanly lit corridor.

He hesitated, his hand on the newel post, and frowned. Whoever it was, they weren't trying to hide. Probably the clerk had been trying to alert him to guests. But the hell of it was, guests were the last things he wanted, even the friendly variety.

He proceeded reluctantly down the corridor. At the door, he stopped and gazed into his room.

Fernanda Salazar was there. She was the one he saw first, because her beauty snatched all illumination in any room and all eyes always went first to her. She wore a mantilla and a white lace dress that clung stunningly along her body. He felt a twinge in his loins, despite his fatigue.

Then he saw Don Hernán Salazar. The grandee sat in a club chair that had obviously been carted in by hotel employees anxious to please the rancher. The chair in which Fernanda sat was less comfortable than the grandee's, but had also added to the room's furnishings, which originally included only a single straight chair.

There was also a small table covered with a linen cloth, silverwear, plates, dishes, glasses, and cups. As they waited, Fernanda and her father sipped at red wine in crystal tumblars.

Nothing in this world like making yourselves at home.

Longarm knocked on the doorjamb and grinned tiredly at them. "May I come in?"

Don Hernán Salazar laughed and stood up. "My dear boy. I hope you don't mind our intruding like this."

"Of course he doesn't Father," Doña Fernanda said, smiling.

Fernanda's brilliantly white, even teeth glittered in the lamplight. She got up and came toward him, her hand extended formally, but her eyes were glowing and he saw that her olive-black eyes were where she stored her hidden meanings.

She touched his hand with her cool, shapely fingers and he felt his loins growing warm again.

"We wanted so much to talk to you, Señor Long," Fernanda said. Her back was to her father and she tipped her tongue across her lips in a tantalizing way.

124

Longarm tried to remain as cool and detached as Fernanda sounded. His gaze touched her mouth and then slid along the slender column of her throat, following the natural pull of gravity. But then something struck him, and his gaze jerked back.

He stared, incredulous, at the cross about her neck. There were millions of gold crosses, but somehow, instinctively, he knew this was the cross Fernanda had lost in the stagecoach robbery. He said, "Your cross—How did you get it back?"

"Isn't that the oddest thing?" Fernanda said. She walked beside him to where her father awaited them. She touched at the cross with the tips of her fingers. "It was returned to me in a plain, sealed envelope. No note. Nothing. I had the chain clasp fixed, and it's as good as new."

He couldn't say why, but somehow that cross added to the strangeness of this entire evening.

Don Hernán Salazar shook hands with Longarm, and then imperiously invited him to sit in the remaining chair. Fernanda returned to her chair, her smiling gaze fastened on Longarm's face. But despite her smiling, he felt the fluttering of wrong stirring in his stomach.

Don Hernán poured him a glass of wine. "From our own vineyards, Señor Long," he said. "The taste—like nectar." He made a kissing sound, and smiled.

Everybody's smiling, Longarm thought. He remembered how W. W. Meriman had smiled at him today in that elegant office. He had bought what Meriman was selling, and now here was the leading rancher of the area, giving him the old pitch. He sipped at the wine, barely aware of its bouquet or taste.

"I came as soon as I heard," Salazar said.

Longarm frowned. "Heard? Heard what, sir?"

"Why, come now, Mr. Long. I hear you are leaving no stone unturned, looking for the principal owners of the Houston-Grant Land Company. Too bad you didn't come directly to me."

Longarm shook his head.

"How did you hear I was looking for these people?" he asked at last.

Don Salazar shrugged. "I think I told you before, Mr. Long.

125

I have the means to learn whatever is important for me to know.."

"But I haven't told anybody except Tom Houghton. And I sent a wire. By Western Union. You own both, Mr. Salazar?"

Don Hernán stood up, his smile expansive. He set his wineglass down carefully and stood gazing down at Longarm. "My dear boy," he said. "Aren't we concerning ourselves with unimportant details?"

"I don't know," Longarm said.

Don Hernán stopped smiling. ."I hope I haven't misunderstood my daughter." He watched Longarm oddly.

Longarm shook his head. "I hope not, sir. About what?"

"Doña Fernanda told me that it was understood between you. It was agreed that you would . . . support us in this matter."

Longarm gazed up at Don Hernán, then shifted his gaze to Fernanda; she watched him with a coolly detached smile. "Right now I'm pretty confused," he said. "But what I think I told Doña Fernanda was that I *hoped* we would be fighting together. I still hope that."

"So do I," Don Hernán said. "I hope we have not misjudged you."

"I don't know how you've judged me. Doña Fernanda suggested that the miners—men like W. W. Meriman—were spoiling this country, poisoning the water. I told her that if the miners—Meriman or anyone else—encroached on your lands, I would be on your side. That's why I'm here."

"The miners certainly are despoiling this lovely land," Fernanda said. "They will turn it into waterless, barren wastes unless we stop them."

"We?" Longarm said in an empty voice. "I reckon you are talking about the Houston-Grant Land Company."

"My daughter and I are principals of the company, along with other ranchers and civic leaders interested in preserving this lovely land."

Longarm swallowed back the bile gorging up in his throat. "And the Border Land Company?"

"I and a consortium of concerned ranchers formed the Border Land Company. Yes."

Longarm felt chilly. He watched the curtains billow at the

126

windows in the cross-draft. "And the Arizona-Santa Fe?" he inquired.

"That is one of our holdings too." Salazar nodded. "As you can see, we are being as open and aboveboard with you as we can be. Arizona-Santa Fe is slightly different from the other two corporations, but its final goal is certainly the same—the preservation of our lands against the encroachment of the mines."

Longarm sighed. "You mind saying what is the main purpose of Arizona-Santa Fe?"

"Certainly not. It is the financing company behind the new Grant County Electric Power Company. I am proud to say that we are selling bonds, making all preparations to bring electric power to Silver City—and eventually to all of Grant County—when and if that is feasible. Perhaps you have seen the electric power plant? It is under construction over on Hudson Street."

Longarm stood with his hands clenched at his sides. He said, "No, I haven't seen it yet. It sounds . . . very progressive. Very civic-minded. That's the hell of it. You people are convinced that what you are doing is right—that the ends justify the means, and that it doesn't matter who gets hurt, as long as you have your way—for the good of the survivors."

"You sound rather cynical, Mr. Long," Don Hernán said. "There have been people hurt. I can't promise there won't be others hurt. But you are right. In the long run, what we are doing will be justified. We are fighting Meriman and his faction, trying to get the Anti–Hydraulic Mining Act through the legislature. Trying to get Washington to act against them. We are backing a full slate of anti-mining-interest candidates in next week's election. The Anti-Mining Act is one of the propositions to be voted on. Meriman's people are running a slate to oppose us, and threatening anyone who dares to vote against them."

"And who is running a slate to represent the *people?*" Longarm inquired. "Who is to look after the interests of the people?"

"Why, sir, I don't even understand your tone! *We* will protect the people. Our candidates will protect the people."

"How?" Longarm said. "When do you start? Will Desdardes Codina have a home left by the time you get around to pro-

127

tecting *him?* You—a holder of Spanish land-grant acreage—you are grabbing lands away from little farmers like Codina!"

Don Hernán stared at Longarm. His dark face grew flushed. He said, "I thought you and Doña Fernanda had discussed this. I thought you understood."

"Mr. Salazar, I don't understand anything. Right now I'm about as confused as a man can get. I'm down here to stop violations of the U.S.-Mexican Treaty of 1848—to stop illegal land grabbing. And you are the leader of the people grabbing up the lands."

"What we are doing is for the good of the land, and of the people. We must own this land—in order to protect it."

"But don't you understand? Why do you stand there, blind to the only important fact in this insanity? *You,* a Spanish grandee, a nine-generations land grant holder—you are violating the treaty that protects *you."*

"I am a strong man, sir. A wealthy man. I need no one—no laws—to protect me. I am strong enough to hold what is mine."

"Yes. *You* are. But what about Desdardes Codina? Ricardo Martinez? They are not strong enough. And it is you who are helping to destroy them."

"I? Destroying? My dear boy, I and all my ancestors have dedicated our lives and devoted our fortunes to protecting and improving this land and the people who belong on it."

"Are you saying Codina and the others don't belong—as you do? They hold—or held—the same kind of grant that protects you."

Don Hernán shrugged. "You are worrying about the wrong things, my boy. The wrong people. Codina and the others will lose their holdings anyway."

"So you just help them along, by wrenching out the heart of their land—that part with good water on it. I don't care how lofty your aims are, Mr. Salazar, your acts are criminal—and in violation of federal laws."

"That's where you are mistaken, sir. The territorial legislature, in its wisdom, has seen fit to pass certain—exemptions—to the Treaty of Guadalupe Hidalgo. And it is under those exemptions that we are acting to preserve this area of southwest New Mexico."

"But the whole thing is illegal. You must know that. The boys in Santa Fe who passed the exemption rules—they've got to know that the treaty with Mexico is federal."

"My dear boy, you are getting exercised over trivialities. I think you will find that states' rights supercede the federal statutes."

Longarm shook his head. "Maybe they do, maybe they don't. But whoever started this land-grabbing did it without bothering to inform Washington and Congress."

Salazar waved his arm. "I think, my dear boy, you will find that what I am doing is quite legal and in the best interests of southwestern New Mexico. And after the election it will be firmly and totally acceptable, according to state or national laws."

"I've seen blind people," Longarm said, "and people who refuse to see, but you have blinded yourself to the truth, Mr. Salazar, and I reckon you better start to undo this mess before I have to arrest you."

Salazar straightened, gripping his cane. "Arrest? Me? Who would dare?"

"I'm afraid I would have to, Mr. Salazar, unless you can undo those illegal land grabs in the next twenty-four hours."

"I think we have no more to say to each other, Mr. Long." Salazar nodded his head toward his daughter, and Fernanda stood up.

"You can't get away with it. Tell him, Fernanda, for God's sake. He's stealing land and water from these people."

Salazar had taken up his impeccable white planter's hat. Now he straightened and turned around.

"I am grabbing nothing. I act according to New Mexican law. I am gathering the water, because with the water I can control what happens to the land. And I shall continue to do that, and neither you, nor anyone else will stop me."

"I'll sure as hell have to try."

"I was hoping you were smarter than this, Mr. Long. I am afraid you will find that opposing me may prove fatal to you."

"Hell," Longarm said, "I've been threatened before."

"Have you, sir?" Salazar walked toward the door, paused and looked back. "Suppose in this case I am not merely threatening you—"

"Sounds like the same old threats to me," Longarm said. He smiled coldly.

"Suppose I am simply stating a fact," Salazar concluded, then stepped ahead of his daughter and touched the knob of the door.

Longarm looked at Fernanda, but the beautiful girl was gazing through him again, as if she had never seen him before, and didn't look forward to encountering him again.

"We are trying so hard to save our beloved land," she said. "And you are trying to stop us."

"Forget him, Doña Fernanda," Don Hernán advised. "He is only one little man, and before this is through, he will find how little he truly is."

Don Hernán Salazar opened the door. He stepped through it and paused to allow his daughter to precede him.

At that moment, Longarm heard a whisper of sound along the corridor—it could have been mice in the wall, litter in the wind, a footstep. But Longarm knew it wasn't.

"Look out!" he yelled.

Don Hernán turned to stare coldly at him. This, and the fact that Doña Fernanda grabbed his arm and yanked him into the room, kept him from getting a bullet in the chest.

Longarm waited only to see Salazar sag down against the doorjamb. The don's fine suit had sprouted a blood-red carnation. People ran out into the hallway and stood staring at the don, who would have fallen except that Doña Fernanda supported him.

Drawing his gun, Longarm ran into the hallway. He pushed people aside and went running down the stairs.

When he came out into the lobby, it too was crowded with people standing as if in a trance, bewitched by the sound of gunfire from upstairs.

The night clerk stood half out in the lobby. His face was taut and bleak.

"Who came off that stairway?" Longarm asked.

The clerk made a visible effort to speak before he was able to say anything. "That little man," the clerk gasped. His voice grew stronger. "That one hanging around—looking for you."

"Banning? J. Z. Banning?"

The clerk nodded. Longarm started past him, then stopped and spoke over his shoulder. "Get Mr. Salazar's driver up to my room to help him. Get him to the hospital if you can."

The night clerk nodded, but did not try to speak. He jerked his head toward the rear door into the alley, and Longarm ran across the room.

At the rear door, Longarm glanced back and the clerk was hurrying up the stairs. He didn't wait to see any more.

Holding his gun in his fist, Longarm turned the knob and eased open the door to the alleyway.

Holding his gun ready before him, Longarm slid through the doorway into the alley. It was as well lit as Main Street, with lamplight spilling through open rear windows and doors.

Papers and debris spilled along the narrow passage on the wind. Longarm pressed against the wall and searched both ways for shadows or movement. He held his breath, waiting. Nothing stirred. Somewhere a cat meowed in the stillness, and then the alleyway was silent again.

Longarm sidled along the alley, going the length of the block, parallel to Main. He checked each space between buildings, looked in every open window. Sometimes faces stared out at him like masks from some horror show but he caught no sign of the runty little Banning.

Finally he reached the corner and turned back. He walked back along the alley, holding his gun at his side. At the hotel, he walked out to the busy cross-street. Market Street was stirring with life. It was like a disturbed anthill, with people hurrying in every direction.

He stood for a long time, looking both ways. There were only the usual sights and noises of the night. He stepped back inside the hotel lobby from the alley door and holstered his gun.

The night clerk had returned to his post behind the desk, where he sat in a kind of trance. A semblance of order had returned to the lobby.

Longarm crossed the lighted lobby and went up the stairs. The long hallway was quiet; the door to his room was closed. It seemed odd that order could be restored so quickly, but he couldn't shake the sense of madness about the whole night.

His door was locked. He found the room key, unlocked it,

131

and stepped inside. He saw where Don Hernán had lost some blood, but it had been scrubbed away; only a dark stain of water remained. The table and extra chairs and the wine were all gone; it was as if Salazar and his daughter had never been here.

He knew better. The room looked as it had before, but nothing was the same.

He looked about. It was as if he had walked into a nightmare where everything was familiar but nothing was as it should be.

Chapter 11

Longarm woke at first light the next morning, his mind churning
with the nightmare he'd walked into last night—Spanish grandee violating the very law that had been designed to protect
him; a rich man talking about saving and improving the en-
vironment, as a cover for buying up all the decent water in the
region. What had Salazar said? *"If I control the water, I can
control what happens to the land."* Hell, if he controlled enough
water, he'd soon *own* all the land. No wonder he didn't believe
he needed an old treaty to protect himself. For all his high-
flown talk, he was walking roughshod over anybody and everybody who got in his way.

Unable to sleep, Longarm got up, washed at the washstand
as well as he could, dressed, and had breakfast in the hotel
dining room. Conversations petered out when he walked in.
People glanced at him covertly, as if measuring him for his
own coffin.

He finished eating, feeling as if the eggs and steak were jammed up tight against his solar plexus, and walked out of the hotel into the tension crackling along the washed-out Main Street.

People behaved as if he were a leper. They crossed the street when they saw him coming. They walked widely around him, or entered the first convenient store. Some even jerked their heads about, looking wildly for cover.

He exhaled heavily. He didn't blame them for being scared. He felt as if he were walking in the morning sunlight with a bright target in the middle of his back.

An open carriage, driven by a derbied man, with a woman and child on the seat beside him, rattled past, drawn by a brown mare. The driver tipped his hat and nodded, but did not speak.

Longarm stopped in the middle of the walk, staring after Judge McLoomis, and his wife, Honoria, and their young son. Their bags and picnic basket were stacked in the tonneau of the carriage.

Longarm's spirits lifted slightly. Judge McLoomis was on his way to Lordsburg to get evidence against the land grabbers. Somebody in this hellhole did give a damn. The judge was trying to help him.

He sighed, feeling slightly less alone.

At the town hospital they told him Don Hernán Salazar had been treated during the night for a flesh wound and released. He had probably returned to his ranch.

He walked back to Main Street, drawing deeply on a cheroot and mentally composing the report he would telegraph to Billy Vail. "Have evidence that should be turned over to the U.S. Attorney." That about said it. He wrote out the telegram, paid for it, and walked out Broadway to the County Building.

Deputy Sheriff Len Hazelton, in shirtsleeves and suspenders, began to shake his head when Longarm walked in. "Why don't you wait to find out what I want?" Longarm inquired.

Hazelton spread his hands. "I don't care what you want. You're poison in this office right now."

"What the hell are you talking about?"

"You. The mine owners are scared of you. The ranchers are

134

dead set against you. The people don't trust you. And we don't need that in this office."

"Isn't this a sheriff's office?"

"It is. But we got our own problems. A sheriff has to be elected. To be elected, he's got to be popular. He can't be involved with a man like you, that everybody hates."

"Just the same, I'd like to talk to Sheriff Whitehill."

Hazelton shook his head. "He's not here. I told you. The sheriff's not in the office much these days."

"Where is he?"

"Why don't you let the sheriff alone until after the election?"

"Because, goddamn it, there are laws being broken in this fouled-up county."

"Listen. Laws were being broken before you came near here. They'll be broken after you're gone. And after the election. Right now, we don't need a wild man from Denver rocking the boat. Sheriff's got eight opponents running against him in the election. He's got to keep things quiet. He's got to stay in good with everybody."

"Where would I find him?"

"How do I know? Out politicking, maybe. I told you, he don't come in the office much."

"Where could I find him right now, at"—Longarm glanced up at the Seth Thomas clock on the wall—"at nine in the morning?"

"Hell, I don't know. Maybe at home."

Sure enough, Longarm found Sheriff Harvey Whitehill sitting in a rocking chair on the front porch of his house on Bullard Street.

The sheriff was a graying man, about five feet seven inches tall. His shoulders were heavy, but he was trim of build, with a soup-strainer mustache and unsmiling eyes. He rocked and smoked, watching Longarm approach.

Longarm ascended the wide front steps to the shaded veranda, which boasted ferns and flowers in pots, rocking chairs, and a swing. The house was well built, on a serene street. Longarm said, "Sheriff Whitehill, I'm Custis Long, deputy U.S. marshal out of Denver."

Whitehill rocked forward and spat tobacco juice into his front yard. He wiped the back of his hand across his mouth and nodded. "Heard of you."

"I've heard of you too," Longarm said. "But I ain't *seen* much of you."

"That so?" Whitehill went on rocking. He didn't invite Longarm to sit down.

"That's right. I arrested one of the town marshal's deputies. He better be in your jail right now."

"He's there." Whitehill went on rocking.

"Another so-called deputy marshal tried to bushwhack me in the hills south of here. He's in the hospital, unless he died during the night. Another deputy marshal shot at me from an alley last night. I may have killed him."

"Heard all that. You're quite a fellow. Reckon you've made more enemies in three days than I've racked up in the past eight years as sheriff."

"Hell, no wonder. You don't do anything but sit on your butt and rock."

"Just temporary, son. In 1875, I was coroner when a man named McIntosh was sheriff. This was a wild frontier town then. McIntosh embezzled three thousand bucks and went to Mexico one night. I was appointed sheriff in his place. Me and my deputy, Dan Tucker, cleaned this place up and made it a good place to live in the past seven, eight years."

"You got troubles right now. Have you gone out of the law-enforcement business?"

The faintest suggestion of a smile tugged at the tobacco-stained corners of the sheriff's mouth. It didn't reach his eyes, and was quickly gone. "Temporarily, Mr. Long. I don't need you or no other government man coming in here, telling me how to run my office. But I'll just say this to you. I been a good sheriff. A damn good sheriff. Much of what this town is, it owes to me. But even if a man's the best lawman in the world, if he's dependent on electors, he's got to be elected, otherwise what he is, or knows, or can do, ain't worth a hoot in hell."

"So you mean to sit on your duff until after the elections?"

"There's a town marshal. He's got full authority inside Sil-ver City."

"You can sit here and pretend not to know it, but that town marshal is as crooked as he is yellow."

"Them's serious charges."

"I know. And you'll look into 'em, as soon as the election is over."

"That's right. If I look into 'em now, and I ain't sheriff after next week, won't do me or the town much good, will it?"

"Jesus." Longarm shook his head. "You know I can't work with a marshal whose deputies are trying to kill me."

"I hear it's open season on you."

"Maybe it is. But you're smart enough to know this town will be crawling with U.S. marshals if I'm killed."

"I'd hope folks will be smart enough to realize that. Why don't you warn the town marshal he ought to pass that word around?"

"Because the marshal's not smart enough to realize it. I've warned Tuttle that the next time one of his deputies attacks me, I'm going to kill Tuttle himself. And I'm advising you of that fact right now."

Whitehill stopped rocking. "My God, Tuttle is helpless to stop those deputies of his from doing *anything*. Why, man, those deputies no more take orders from Tuttle than—than you do."

Longarm shrugged. "That's *his* problem."

Whitehill resumed rocking. "You are one tough hombre, ain't you?"

Longarm spoke in savage exasperation. "Let's just say I've got a tough job and I'm still alive. This is your town, Sheriff. Don't you give a shit about what happens to it?"

"I do care, son. That's why I'm doing my damnedest to get reelected. If I'm *ex*-Sheriff Whitehill, this town can go to hell, and nothing I can do about it."

"A known killer who wears notches on his gun, a punk named J. Z. Banning, wanders these streets. Last night he almost killed Hernán Salazar. He may have been trying to kill me, or he might have been trying to kill Salazar. Reckon that depends on who hired him. You mean you can't send a deputy to arrest him for attempted murder?"

"We'll arrest him, if we can. Meantime, that's something you ought to take up with Marshal Tuttle."

"Banning thinks Billy the Kid is coming back here to this town. That's how low this place has sunk."

Whitehill shook his head, remembering. "Hell, Billy the Kid ain't coming back here. We all know Billy. Reckon I got the dubious honor of being the first lawman ever to arrest Billy. He robbed a Chinese laundry downtown here. I locked him up for it. He was just a kid and I was just trying to scare him. I was going to let him think it over and then I was going to let him out, but he climbed out the chimney—a boy his size, he could do that easy. He caught a freight wagon and went from here to Fort Grant, Arizona. He killed a blacksmith over there who thought he was Billy's best friend. Heard a lot about the Kid since then."

"So's everybody," Longarm said. "Banning means to shoot it out with Billy, when and if the Kid comes back to Silver City. You going to arrest Billy again?"

"We'll cross that bridge when we get to it."

"After the election."

"After the election. I'm staying out of these controversial matters as much as I can, Long. I got friends—and votes—on both sides of every question."

"That means I can't count on you—or your office—for anything."

Whitehill chewed and rocked for a moment. At last he nodded and gazed at Longarm expressionlessly. He leaned forward, spat, and wiped his hand across his mustache, then smiled coldly, staring straight into Longarm's eyes. "You finally figured it out, Mr. Long."

Enraged, Longarm strode along Bullard Street. For the moment he felt too tired and frustrated to do anything. At the Western Union office on Main, he asked if there was a response to his telegram to Governor Wallace. There was none.

Sighing, he went into the nearest barbershop. The barbers looked ill. None wanted to shave him. Finally the man at the last chair took his life in his hands and lathered up Longarm's face, with fingers that trembled visibly.

Longarm lay back and closed his eyes. The hot water and lather felt good. He was afraid the trembling barber was going to slit his throat, but at this moment, one way of dying seemed like any other.

He went back over all the nightmarish events that had enshrouded him in the days since he'd arrived in Silver City. There had to be a way out. Finally he decided he had the answer.

The barber was saying, "All finished, Mr. Long. I tell you, I admire a cool customer like you, lying there almost asleep. Man could have walked in here and—" He jerked the striped cloth away and stared at the gun lying ready in Longarm's hand. The barber's eyes widened and he backed away. "Oh my God," he said, shaking his head. "Oh my God."

The Silver City *Enterprise* office was a large, single-storied, yellow adobe building, with a brick fringe along the roofing and five brick chimneys. It sat within a fence, with a long, slick hitch rail and a water trough out front, on a corner lot.

His rage building, Longarm stalked into the front office. The place was quiet. A woman sat alone at a rolltop desk in the space that was separated from the printing office by a slatted fence about three feet high, with a swinging gate in it. Beyond the fence, Longarm saw one man working alone at a makeup block.

"Yes?" the woman said, and Longarm brought his gaze back to her. She looked harried and somewhat disheveled, with tendrils of her dark brown hair spilling loose from her hairpins and dripping in damp little curls over her forehead. What she looked most of all was surprisingly pretty, with gentle features, a full-lipped mouth, and upslanted violet eyes behind rimless glasses.

"May I help you?" she asked.

"I hope so," he said fervently. "I'm looking for the editor of this newspaper."

"I'm the editor." She removed her glasses, and her upslanted eyes gleamed lovelier than ever.

"Holy God," Longarm whispered.

"What's the matter?"

"Nothing. Isn't anything in this town the way it is in the real world?" Longarm shook his head in exasperation.

"You mean most editors are crusty old men."

"Most of them I've met, yes ma'am."

"What was it you wanted to see me about?"

Longarm exhaled. "Ma'am, I know from looking at you that your newspaper publishes recipes for the best rhubarb pie in the West. But I was looking for something else."

"You're not being very fair, are you, judging me before you give me a chance? What do you want?"

Longarm shook his head. "Before I tell you, ma'am, please tell me one thing. What's your lead story in the *Enterprise* this week?"

Her face colored slightly, and the coloring added to her fragile beauty. "The lead story is about the condition of Main Street."

"That's what I thought."

"Don't you think that's an important story? Don't you think the county commissioners and the city council ought to get together and do something about it, before half the town is washed away?"

"Something ought to be done, all right," Longarm admitted.

"That's just what I'm saying. I'm pulling no punches. You know how Main Street began to be torn up by flooding in the first place?"

"It looks like a creekbed. It looks like water that used to be held in the mountains by the trees runs down through it because the trees have all been cut down."

"Very good. That's the basic reason. But there are other reasons far more urgent—and maybe even criminal. The houses and walks made the street like a river channel. When floodwater from the mountains poured through, it began to take part of it away. The annual floods found the weak spots in the adobe soil, especially at the end of the town, where Main Street ends at the edge of a rocky arroyo. Gradually it tore that part away. The city has poured thousands of dollars into ripraps to hold back the floods, but nothing helps. And do you know why?"

"No ma'am, I don't."

"Because once this flat had no deep washes; it was very level and unbroken. The soil is a heavy loam, and that spread out the floods over the entire area. But just south of Broadway, on Main Street, mind you, builders dug a huge adobe hole. Do you know why? Of course you don't. Adobes were made— on the spot—for the building that houses Dr. Bailey's Drugstore at the southwest corner of Main and Broadway. Ever since then, water has been eating away at the street, and nobody has been able to stop it."

"You do sound as if you get real incensed by stupidity and criminality."

"I certainly do."

"Well, that's why I'm here. I'd like you to do a story that the people ought to know. Before the election. It's about stupidity and criminality at least as bad as tearing up Main Street to build a drugstore."

"My name is Claudia O'Neill," the editor said. "What's yours?"

"Custis Long."

She laughed and handed him a proof sheet with the layout for a column-length story. "Oh yes," she said, "I've heard all about you."

He stared at the headlines:

U.S. MARSHAL ARRIVES

Arrests One Town Deputy; Two Wounded; Chief Marshal Threatened

Locks Town Marshal in Own Cell

"You've been busy," she said, smiling archly.

"I haven't even started yet. But I find there is a price on my head."

"I heard that."

"But you didn't run it in your story?"

"I couldn't substantiate it."

"They're shooting at me for some reason. I figure it's for profit, since they don't know me well enough yet to hate me."

"And what's the story you think I ought to run?"

"I can't fight people I don't know. I can't fight gunslicks I can't see. But you can tell the people the truth about what's going on here in this town."

"And what truth is that?"

"Well, let's start easy. You've got a sheriff who may once have been a ball of fire. But he's interested in nothing now but staying in office. He sits on his tail and does nothing until after the election."

"That might be a good way to elect somebody else, but I happen to think Sheriff Whitehill has done a lot for this town."

"Well, he's not doing anything right now." Longarm's voice shook with rage.

She gazed up at him. "Anything else?"

"The mines are dumping their slag down slopes and in creeks and poisoning the water of the people who are living below them."

"Is that all?"

"No. There are land companies grabbing land. That may not be news, but what is news is that part of that land is protected by U.S. treaties, and that makes it a federal crime."

"You are angry, aren't you?"

"I'm just trying to do my job, ma'am. And the only way I can do that is to stay alive. The only way I can stay alive is to wake people up to what's going on. A sheriff who holds his job by refusing to act at all. A useless town marshal whose deputies are paid killers hired by people in power, people whose names I don't know yet—for sure."

"And you think putting all that in my newspaper will help you do your job?"

"Don't you care that there's an election coming up, but there are people, like Desdardes Codina, who have been warned they'll be killed if they try to vote? Don't you give a damn that the miners threaten riots if the voters pass the Anti–Hydraulic Mining Act referendum ?"

"I care," she said. "I care deeply. But do you know how many people work here? I work here. And my printer, Al Huckworth, back there. I don't mind dying for what I believe, but I don't think I have the right to endanger Al Huckworth's life. But he is the printer, and I couldn't get this paper out without him."

"Then you won't do anything either?"

She stood up and replaced her glasses on the bridge of her

142

nose. "Stop trying to push me. I don't know yet what I'll do. But before you get enraged at me for being just a little cautious, maybe I ought to tell you, I am the *widow* O'Neill."

"I'm sorry to hear that."

"I'm not asking for your sympathy, Mr. Long. I'm just placing all the facts before you. One fact is that when my husband took over this newspaper—which had failed and gone out of business in 1875—when Ephraim took it over, it became the most lucrative and well-read paper in the territory. Only one thing was wrong." She got up and found a newspaper in a file behind her. She tossed it on the desk, facing Longarm. "Ephraim was killed—for the *facts* he published. You can get me killed for publishing *facts* that certain people don't want published. Do you want that?"

He stared down at the newspaper, which recounted how nightriders had attacked the editor in his office, slain him, and ridden away. They had neither been apprehended nor punished. The crime had gone unsolved. He sighed heavily. "Just forget it, ma'am. I don't want to get anybody killed. Especially not two people as pretty as you and Al Huckworth."

She almost smiled. She removed her glasses again. She said, "Ephraim wasn't totally blameless, however."

"Oh?"

"Ephraim was a good man. I think he was too good. He was extremely religious. He was holier-than-thou. He didn't mean to be, he was just a Down East New England puritan, and he couldn't help it. He fearlessly printed the shortcomings of everyone—including infidelities, and even the names of men seen entering Miss Nellie Pyles' Fandango Saloon."

"So almost anybody might have killed him."

"Almost everyone wanted to," she agreed.

Longarm sighed and nodded. "So you've run a kind of middle-of-the-road newspaper since then, eh?"

"That's right. I've done what I could. I'm going to get Main Street fixed before it's too late—if I can. I fight against poisoning the water in every issue. You may as well know, I've been warned not to oppose either side in this election."

"Do you get the idea this whole town's gone crazy?"

"There's a lot of money at stake," she said. "And money

143

makes people do weird things to each other."

The front door was thrown open and a youth ran in, panting. "A dollar for a news break, Miss Claudia? I got one for you. Sheriff's deputies are gettin' up a posse right now. Word just come in from the south stage road to Lordsburg. Judge McLoomis, his wife and son. They're all dead. They been scalped by Injuns."

Chapter 12

A dozen men were milling around the massacre site when Longarm got there, riding fast on a livery-rented roan.

Before he glanced toward the murdered family, Longarm ground-tied his mount at the edge of the winding roadway and went directly to the sheriff.

"Aren't you going to rope off this area? You've got to keep people out of here. Half of Silver City is on its way out here. You get enough people trampling around here afoot and on horses, you won't ever be able to find out what happened."

Sheriff Whitehill winced. He objected neither to Longarm's tone nor to his telling him how to conduct a murder investigation. He said only, "Oversight, Long. I'm gut-sick about ol' Lynch McLoomis. Without him, there's no honesty in that County Building." He shook his head, as if physically shaking off the despair that threatened to swamp him. In minutes, ropes were strung across the road and tied to trees enclosing the site of the murders.

It was easy to see why the sheriff was sick to his stomach, beyond losing the last totally dedicated law official in the county.

The McLoomis family had been murdered at a curve in a climbing roadway. Oaks and underbrush grew among the rocks and boulders in a heavily wooded area above Thompson's Canyon. There were plenty of places to hide; a dry creekbed ran through the trees toward the edge of the canyon.

The carriage horse had been killed in its traces and lay where it had fallen between the shafts. The eight-year-old boy lay dead in the bed of the carriage, where Longarm had seen picnic basket and suitcases when the family left Silver City. Bags and baskets were gone, a kind of proof that they were dealing with, as one man kept saying, "thievin', murderin' Apaches."

"We begged that son of a bitch Hatch to send troops to protect us. Hell, no. His troops were exhausted, he couldn't spare the men. Now look what's happened."

"Hell, Governor Wallace is no better. We begged him for help against the Apaches, and what did he send us, for Christ's sake—thirty-six goddamn army rifles!"

"I tried to wire Washington to complain about Hatch. Hell, my telegram never even got there."

"They say Hatch has started censoring all military wires."

"Is Western Union a military wire?"

"It is in time of trouble with Indians."

"How you going to get the truth out of here, if'n Hatch don't want you to?"

Longarm stopped listening and concentrated on the scene of slaughter.

The eight-year-old child had been stripped and scalped, and his body mutilated. It looked as if Mrs. McLoomis had tried to run into the surrounding oaks. Her body lay just inside the first ring of trees, facedown, naked. The back of her head had been blown away.

The judge's body was about two hundred yards to the south. He had been shot in four places. Along the way were the clear signs of the kind of struggle the man had waged against the murderers. Plainly, he had fought to save the carriage and child.

It was clear that he had retreated slowly, maybe already shot once or twice. They had jumped him and he had fought free. He'd stopped, loaded his gun, fired it, and retreated again, until he was killed. Like his wife and child, the judge had been stripped and robbed—even his shoes were gone—but he had not been mutilated.

"It's some kinda code with them damned wild Apaches," somebody said. "Apaches don't mutilate a brave enemy—even if'n he's white."

Longarm walked away. Men were trampling through the trees and underbrush. He cursed them silently. Unless he worked fast, every true clue as to what had happened here would be lost.

He heard sounds of horses' hooves and carriage wheels and people shouting from the roadway, as the curious arrived from Silver City.

He thanked God that Sheriff Whitehill had sense enough to keep the sensation-seekers behind the ropes.

He kept pacing between the trees, along the dry creekbed, and even on the roadway. There had been a lot of traffic up here since the judge and his family had been slain, but there was not one sign of an unshod horse.

He remarked on this to Whitehill, who swore and growled from deep in his throat, "Jesus, man. It was Apaches, all right. Is any white man inhuman enough to do what's been done here today?"

Longarm shrugged. "I've found hoofprints. But I've not found one sign of unshod horses."

Whitehill yelled for three of his best trackers. "I want you men to drop everything else. Find where the killers tied their horses."

The men fanned out. Figuring that the killers had been in high ground, from which they could watch for the approaching carriage up the inclined road, Longarm went up the hill, looking for level ground and a good lookout site.

He found the place where they'd waited. There were boot-prints in the hard ground, and he found half a dozen cigarette butts. By the minute he became more certain that there had been no Apaches in this area. He put the butts in his jacket pocket and went deeper into the rocks and trees.

He walked into an aspen clump and found where horses had been tied and left. He studied the ground carefully. There could be no mistake. Every horse wore shoes, and a couple of them were the heavy kind used by the cavalry.

He straightened, his heart slugging. He glanced downhill through the trees. He saw the curiosity-seekers lined along the ropes at the edge of the road. He saw Whitehill and his deputies at work in the copse of trees.

He decided not to report his find yet. No sense getting the site trampled until he had a chance to look it over. He didn't find much—a few more cigarette butts, places where men and animals had relieved themselves. Then he spotted something fluttering in a chokecherry bush.

He went to the bush and carefully removed the folded paper that had blown against the jagged limbs and become entangled there.

It was the front page and the following three pages of a newspaper: the Council Bluffs *Leader*. The paper was crumpled, folded, and torn, but it had not been up here long enough to yellow.

He scanned it, and found something at the top corner. Smoothing the paper out, he found a printed address that was almost obliterated. Mr. H. C. Cohen, Cohen's Department Store, Broadway, Silver City, New Mexico.

As if he'd discovered treasure, Longarm folded the paper carefully and tucked it in the breast pocket of his coat.

He carefully examined the area for another ten minutes, but found nothing more of interest. Then he walked back up on the roadway and called to the sheriff.

The Cohen Building was a two-storied adobe and stone structure just west of Dr. Bailey's Drugstore at the corner of Broadway and Main.

Longarm walked in in midafternoon; the store seemed pitch black after the brilliant sunlight of the street. The smells of fresh fabrics, perfumes, leather footwear, and notions blended into a pleasant aroma.

A stout woman measured print cloth behind a long counter at the left side of the well-stocked store, which boasted an open balcony across the upper rear. There were no customers in the store at this hour. The stout woman stopped working and smiled at Longarm. "Could I help you, sir? Something nice for your wife? Shoes and men's wear are at the rear. I'll be glad to show you—"

"I'm looking for Mr. H. C. Cohen."

"Mr. Cohen is upstairs, at the rear of the balcony. You'll find him at a desk behind the ladies' corsets section."

Longarm grinned at her. "I don't blame him. A strategic place to watch things."

She frowned, suspecting a joke, but not getting it. He thanked her and started up the wide staircase to the balcony.

It was so quiet in the store that Cohen had heard his clerk talking with Longarm at the front. He came hurrying between the high-packed, fresh-smelling aisles of ladies' hats, dresses, and undergarments.

Cohen was a dark, slender man only a couple of inches over five feet tall, dressed flashily in the sort of checked suit favored by traveling salesmen—which Cohen had undoubtedly been, in his earlier years. He was graying, nearing fifty, but he walked spryly and smiled broadly, sporting a diamond ring on his pinky and a diamond stickpin in his bright red tie. His spats were natty, his shoes gleamingly polished.

"I'm H. C. Cohen," he said, extending his manicured hand. "In what way may I help you, sir?"

Longarm told the merchant his name and asked, "You ever live in Council Bluffs, Iowa, Mr. Cohen?"

"Indeed I did. It was ten years or so ago. Had a notions store there. Went into business for myself when I had enough of boardinghouse cooking and traveling on sooty trains. I did pretty well in Council Bluffs. We were one of the only Jewish families in the town, but we were well accepted, and got along fine. There wasn't any synagogue in town, of course, so my wife and children and I went to the Presbyterian Church. I was on the vestry, you know. A fine town."

"And you subscribe to the newspaper to keep in touch?" Longarm suggested.

H. C. Cohen nodded, beaming.

"That's right," he said. "Exactly right, Mr. Long. I liked the town, and the people. Mostly I read the paper now for the obituaries. Seems most of the folks I knew are passing away. Most every edition, there's another old friend being laid away. Sad. But I like to keep in touch."

"Ever use the newspapers here in your store—to wrap up packages maybe?"

Cohen flushed slightly, then nodded. "Old habit of mine, Mr. Long. Waste not, want not. You can't go against your upbringing. I don't like to waste anything. We have nice wrappings, but sometimes—for bulky things—I will use an old newspaper. I don't want you to think I'm less than successful here in Silver City. It's been wonderful here. I heard about the big silver strikes back in the early seventies. I figured if this wasn't another ghost town—like Shakespeare, south of here, down near where Lordsburg is now—it would be the ideal site for the kind of big department store I always longed to own. Still, I don't like to waste things—even old newspapers."

"Likely, though, you're the only one working in this store who still uses newspapers for wrapping packages?"

Cohen smiled. "Oh, yes. My clerks, they all use the nice paper—has our name printed right on it."

"I might be asking too much of your memory, Mr. Cohen, but in the last day or so, did you wrap anything in a newspaper?" He removed the folded sheet carefully from his inner pocket and spread it out on the counter. "Say, this particular newspaper?"

The little merchant bent over the newspaper and studied it for some moments in the way a seer might pore over tea leaves in a cup. He began to nod his head. "Yes. I do remember. I sold a kitchen knife. Fellow wanted the sharpest one I had in stock. Took a long time getting just the blade and handle he wanted. To protect his hands, I wrapped the knifeblade in this newspaper, wrapped it good and secure so he shouldn't cut himself."

"Do you remember what he looked like?"

"Oh, yes. He'd been in before. And that day he spent a lot of time selecting the knife he wanted, so I'm not likely to forget. He's a soldier from out at Fort Bayard. A black man, name of . . . George Jefferson. That's right. You know the Ninth Regiment out at Fort Bayard is all black soldiers? Did you know that?"

Claudia O'Neill was busily scribbling on scrap newsprint at her desk in the *Enterprise* office. She glanced up at Longarm and smiled bleakly. "I write up the reports on the Apache massacre of the poor McLoomis family just as fast as they come in. Isn't it the saddest thing you ever heard?"

"It's sad," Longarm agreed. "But I wouldn't play up the Apache angle too strong."

"Why, Sheriff Whitehill himself said it was Apaches."

Longarm scowled. "Sheriff Whitehill *wants* it to be Apaches. He doesn't like to believe that the white men he walks among every day, and depends on for their votes and all, could be as vicious and inhuman as these killers."

"He said the McLoomises were robbed. Their picnic lunch and their suitcases were stolen."

"Yes. And their horse was killed. Apaches would have taken the horse—to eat."

She winced slightly. "Maybe they were trying to stop Mr. McLoomis."

"They could have stopped him without killing his horse in the shafts. They're hungry. I know that. They would have taken the horse. And anyway, whoever killed the McLoomises rode horses with shod hooves."

"And Apache ponies don't have shoes."

"You got it. Somebody wants it to *look* like an Apache massacre. And maybe you'd be asking for trouble to say it wasn't." He shrugged. "Hell, run the story the way the sheriff gives it to you."

"But you don't believe it?"

"I know better. I happen to know why McLoomis was going to Lordsburg. Maybe somebody else knew too, and stopped him—and made it look like rampaging Apaches."

She shook her head. "Now I don't know what to write."

"You stay out of trouble. Just write what the sheriff tells you."

She bit her lip. "I feel so cowardly—but I do know that Ephraim had written something the mining people warned him

151

not to touch. But Ephraim was so stubborn. Threatening him was not the way to keep anything out of his newspaper. He printed the story. The night it came out . . . he was killed."

"You better play it safe—you've got to go on living around here. I don't. You've got to stay in business."

"And who do you think killed the judge and his family?"

"Hell, I say hired white killers—or hired killers, anyway. You decide what you want to print."

She drew a deep breath. "No, I won't be cowardly. I'll print your version of the story. I'll quote you."

He shrugged. "That's fair enough, they're already shooting at me."

"By the way, speaking of cowardly, guess who was on the morning train, leaving Silver City forever?"

"I don't know."

"Town Marshal Herm Tuttle and his family. They hid in the station until just before the train pulled out. Then they ran out and boarded the train. He said he is never coming back here."

"Are you printing that?"

"On the front page of the special edition I'm getting out on the McLoomis murders." She put her head back and gazed up at him. "What was it you wanted me to publish—the first time you came in here?"

"I know more now than I did when I first came in here. I also think you are a beautiful lady, and I wouldn't want to be the reason you got in trouble with these people."

"All right. But if you could get something printed, what would it be? Off the record, of course."

He gazed down at her, grinning coldly. "Off the record? I'll tell you what I'd like to see. A three-column editorial on the front page. Something like this in the headline: 'Did Judge McLoomis Die in Vain? Will Your Vote on Tuesday Be in Vain?' Suggest—just suggest—that maybe Judge McLoomis might have been on his way to get sworn proof against criminal activity in high places in Grant County. Then I'd drop that. Let it end right there. Then I would say there are two groups of candidates up for election on Tuesday next. One slate represents the miners and the mining interests. The other bunch is loyal only to the ranchers. The miners and the big ranching interests are well represented in the coming election. But who represents the average voter?

"There is one way to beat the special interests—I'd say that next. There is one way to stop either the miners or the ranchers from controlling your lives. Get out and vote. Don't let threats or fears intimidate you.

"And don't vote for either slate on the ballot, unless there is a good man among them. Write in your own choice. Vote for your own man who will represent the town and the people. Vote out the rascals. Vote for your own better future."

She stared up at him, surprised. "Why, Mr. Long, that's beautiful. I just wish I had the courage to print something like that in my newspaper."

Chapter 13

Fort Bayard was enclosed in adobe-and-brick walls in the hills above Silver City, on the road to Pinos Altos.

Longarm arrived there as the supper fires were beginning to blaze around the fort, and just as General Edward Hatch was going off duty.

General Hatch was reluctant to talk to Longarm, but when he saw the Department of Justice badge, he shrugged and told him to come on into his office.

General Hatch's office was at least the equal of anything in the War Department at Washington, D.C. It was furnished with thick carpeting, sturdy and expensive office furniture, deep chairs, and a leather-covered lounge. An officers' conference table and chairs were lined against an inner wall.

It angered the general that some people—in newspapers and even in the War Department—referred to him as "Colonel" Hatch. He had risen to the rank of brigadier general during the Civil War and had been awarded the rank of major general in 1867.

The general slumped ungraciously behind his desk. The first thing he said was, "I hope you're not here about that Indian trouble."

"What Indian trouble is that, General?"

"Hell, man. Any of it. I got a bellyfull of it—on any front. We've had nothing but Indian raids and atrocities since Victorio first refused to keep his Apaches on the San Carlos Indian reservation because he had some silly notion that we whites expected him to live among Indians he considered lower than dogs. Damnation, man, I can tell you they're *all* lower than dogs, and ought to be exterminated down to the last woman and child."

Longarm smiled faintly. "I hear that's a little easier said than done, General Hatch, even with all the forces at your command."

Hatch sat forward, enraged. "All *what* forces at my command? My armies are run ragged chasing those bastard Apaches through these hills and across the Rio Grande. My Ninth Regiment—all black, you know—is riddled with malcontents, its morale is low, they're run until they can't run anymore. I keep telling these goddman people out here I'm doing the best I can with what I've got."

"I'm sure you are, General."

Hatch sighed, pleased to hear one kind word in a sea of complaints, civilian and military. "Well, thank you."

"It's just that from what I've seen of the Apaches, you couldn't run them down if you had all the cavalry forces west of the Mississippi at your command."

"What the hell are you saying? That we can't wipe out a bunch of starving, sneaking, thieving redskins?"

Longarm grinned coldly. "I'm saying, sir, if General Lee had had Chato and his fighters among his troops, you'd likely be in some Confederate Army prison now."

General Hatch stood up, quivering. "That's blasphemy, sir."

"No, sir. Just hardscrabble fact."

"Why, I was decorated many times for my exploits during the War of Secession. The South could not possibly have won the late war."

"I agree. I'm just suggesting that with Cochise's Chiricauhuas, they might have kept guerrilla action going for another hundred years."

"You're a government man, a federal government man? Your talk is downright traitorous."

Longarm shrugged. "Forgive me, sir. I don't mean to upset you. I'm not here to talk about big war at all, except to say you did indeed make a distinguished name for yourself—"

"Yes, sir. I don't think I'm being immodest when I say I did indeed." He glanced at the clock on the wall. "It's getting late, sir, do you mind stating your business?"

"I'm here on two matters, sir, both of them urgent. I hope you will agree that the second comes under your jurisdiction. Without your help there will be trouble."

"Don't count on anything from this post, sir. Not at this time. We are understaffed, spread too thin, with too many demands being made on us."

"Well, at least on the first matter, I'm sure you can give me the help I need. I came directly to you because I knew you could give the command and I'd be given assistance. It's really a simple matter. I am looking for a soldier, a Private George Jefferson. I want him on a murder charge. That's why I came to you. If he's here, I'll want him locked up in the stockade. I also want to question him about others who might be involved."

Hatch stared at Longarm a long moment, started to speak, then changed his mind. He pressed a button under his desktop and the door was opened immediately. He said, "Is Lieutenant Pershing still in his office? If he is, send him in here."

The door was closed and then opened again almost at once. A tall, slender young second lieutenant entered the room. He was brown-haired, tall, and gleaming with West Point polish not yet rubbed off by the abrasive life of the Western frontier. "I was just leaving, sir. I heard you call for me."

Hatch nodded. "This here is Deputy U.S. Marshal Custis Long, Lieutenant. Says he has a murder warrant for a nigger in your outfit. Name's George Jefferson."

"I think he was one of the killers of Judge Lynch McLoomis and his family, south of Silver City today," Longarm said.

"Impossible," Hatch said. "All reports say that was an Apache attack."

"Yes, sir, I know that. But I'd like to talk to Private George Jefferson."

Hatch shrugged. "That's up to Lieutenant Pershing."

"We'll find him on the rolls and go talk to him," Pershing agreed. "That can't bend any rules."

"See that you don't, Pershing," Hatch said. "We got too many troubles here to let the civilians start pushing us around." He took up his hat and swagger stick and started around the desk. "Oh? What was that second matter?" He grinned coldly. "Maybe I can turn you down on that now and save us all a lot of time."

"It's not a request at all, General Hatch," Longarm said. "It's more of a suggestion. You don't have to give me any answer. I just hope you'll think about it. There's going to be an election in Silver City on Tuesday, and it looks like there might be some violations of federal law. If you were to send a company of soldiers from the fort in there, just their presence might quiet it down."

"I don't mind giving you my answer right now," General Hatch said. "Hell, no. We don't have the men to spare."

He nodded toward them and strode from the room.

Black Jack Pershing set his hat on his head. "Let's see if we can find Private Jefferson on the rolls. I don't know the name myself. I haven't been here long enough to know all the men, though apparently General Hatch does."

The sergeant in charge of personnel remembered George Jefferson without looking him up. "Discharge," he said. "Bad conduct. Just before you got here, Lieutenant Pershing. Last I heard of Jefferson, he was working as a line rider for the Gila River Cattle Company."

Longarm thanked them and started from the adobe building. The sun was setting and the parade ground seemed to burn orange in the strange dusk light. Pershing followed Longarm out of the office. Longarm shook his hand and thanked him. Pershing said, "I'll just walk to the front gate with you. Unless you'll stay for supper as my guest?"

"I reckon I better get back. I want to look up the Gila River Cattle Company and see if I can locate Jefferson, if he hasn't skipped the country."

Pershing nodded. "I understand. On that other matter, Long—I can't promise you, but maybe we can have a platoon or two on view in Silver City on Tuesday."

Longarm laughed and shook his head. "I appreciate your-trying, but I don't want to get you in trouble with General Hatch."

"Oh no." Pershing shook his head and smiled. "I admit I can't get *any* troops into town to guard against riots or vote fraud. General Hatch has closed that door, and we'll just have to accept it. But something I learned at West Point, Long, or maybe it was back when I was teaching high school in Missouri. I learned that when you can't get a thing done for one reason, you give it another name and you end up with what you needed in the first place."

Longarm laughed. "Lieutenant Pershing, something tells me you're going far in this man's army, if they don't court-martial you first for destroying government property."

"Destroying government property? Me?"

"Yeah. A few miles of red tape."

It was deep dark by the time Longarm rode back down onto the flatland and into Silver City. He kept grinning, remembering Pershing's suggestion that they find a new and acceptable reason for putting Fort Bayard troops in Silver City on voting day. Still, he'd recognized Hatch as a harried, overworked man under killing pressures. Hatch had been an outstanding general in the Civil War. But out here, opposing the Apaches who struck and ran, struck and ran, and then came back when you were too tired to raise your gun, he was inept and impotent. To hide the depths of his failure against the Indians, Hatch had banned military telegraphy—which included *all* wires—in order to protect himself. He was daily sending false reports to Washington and bringing charges against anyone who opposed him. Longarm admired Black Jack Pershing, but he had little faith that the young lieutenant would be any match for the arrogant and bedeviled general.

Shadows flickered, melted, and blended within shadows. Longarm stayed alert, watching men who moved furtively into alleys or who stepped into darkened doorways as he passed. Tension in the town had intensified; this was clear even in the deepest night.

He looped his lines over the leather-slicked hitch rail next door to the brilliantly illumined and brassily noisy Fandango. He didn't see Miss Nellie on her veranda.

He entered the Western Union office and composed a telegram to Governor Wallace, telling him of Hatch's refusal to supply troops to preserve public order on election day, and asking the governor to override the general in this matter.

Less than hopeful, he left the Western Union, reutrned the horse to the Bullard Street livery, and then walked back across Market to the Exchange Hotel.

As he entered the lobby, J. Z. Banning got up from a deep chair near a potted palm and scurried across the carpeting, intercepting Longarm before he reached the desk.

Longarm stared at Banning, shaking his head. "What the hell you doing around here?" he asked.

"It's a free country, Long. I heard how you accused me of shooting at Don Hernán Salazar."

Longarm shrugged. "I had an eyewitness's word on it."

"No you didn't, Long. You had the word of the clerk that he saw me come off the stairway. He didn't say he saw me shooting at nobody. Because I didn't shoot at nobody. The town marshals talked to me, and they talked to the hotel clerk. And they cleared me."

"Congratulations."

"Listen. I still got an urgent message for you." He glanced around the lobby. "Why don't we step out back?"

Longarm laughed in the punk's face. "You've been cleared by the town marshals, Banning. Only the town marshals *haven't* been cleared. I've got one message for *you*. You get out of this town while you're still alive."

J. Z. Banning's face flushed red, then paled as if all the blood had drained from his head. His eyes flashed wildly and his hands trembled out beside his gun.

"Go ahead, coyote," Longarm said. "Draw. Either draw right now, or turn and walk out of here."

Banning's mouth quivered. His eyes blinked and he glanced around the lobby. His gaze touched for a moment at Longarm's cold face, then fell away. He swallowed his Adam's apple. "We'll meet again, Long. Don't you fret that."

Longarm shrugged. Banning backed away a few steps, then turned and strode out of the hotel without looking back.

Longarm exhaled heavily and went up the stairs. Again the door to his room stood open, light spilling into the dimly lit corridor.

Longarm strode along the corridor. He did not slow down. The single precaution he took was to draw his Colt and to hold the gun negligently at his side.

He took two steps inside his room and stopped. The place seemed empty at first, but at a whisper of sound from behind his half-open door, he spun around and stared into the snout of a gun, fixed unwaveringly on him.

His eyes widening in disbelief, he stared at Eastwood Tyne. "What the hell are you doing here?" he said. "I thought I put you in the hospital."

Tyne slammed the door and stood between it and Longarm. "You ain't dealing with no Herm Tuttle now," Tyne said.

"No. Tuttle was smart enough to get out of town."

"Tuttle was a joke. I'm the new town marshal, Long. Oh, I'm still hurt. My belly is still wrapped tight. But they offered me Tuttle's place and I took it."

"Hell, that proves it. You get rid of a bad marshal, that don't always mean you improve things."

"I got the word for you, Long. You be on a stage or on the train tomorrow morning, or my men have word to shoot you on sight."

"You didn't learn a damn thing lying in that hospital bed, did you?" Longarm said. "This is nothing personal, Tyne. You kill me, and you'll have U.S. marshals on you like fleas."

"Maybe, maybe not. If we get you, Long, it will be because you broke a law. That will be our report to the government."

"Going to start shooting men for spitting on the street, eh, Tyne?"

Tyne shrugged. "If we have to. We want you out of here. We want you out of here before the election. Be smart, man. You don't have just the mining people or the ranching people against you. You got the whole town."

"I'm here to do a job, Tyne. I'm not leaving. You'll have to kill me to stop me."

"Don't think I won't. We've already sent a report to the Department of Justice on your false arrest, and your brutal attack on poor Beak Hawes."

"What false arrest is that, Tyne?"

"The man you called Dan Watson. His name is Slim Wheeler, and I've taken him out of the sheriff's custody."

"Figured you needed another gun, huh, Tyne?"

"I don't have to explain myself to you, Long. Our reports show a lawman gone bad—taking bribes. You're through here, Long. We want you out of this town."

A light and yet insistent rap on the door behind Tyne startled him. He jerked his head around.

In that precise instant, Longarm drove his left fist into Tyne's bandaged belly. Tyne's face went gray and he staggered. He tried to turn, and Longarm struck him across the jaw with all the strength he could put behind his fist.

Tyne folded up and sank to the floor. Catching him by the boot heels, Longarm dragged the marshal to the Market Street window. The knock was repeated, but he ignored it. He lifted Tyne's inert body and shoved him headfirst through the window.

Tyne struck the courtesy roof and rolled along it, then off it, striking the ground like a sack of potatoes.

Longarm turned and crossed the room to the door, still holding his gun at his side. "Who is it?" he asked through the facing.

"Could I talk to you, Mr. Long?" It was a woman's voice, which, at that moment, still boiling with rage, Longarm didn't recognize. He heard people yelling from Market Street below his open window, but he ignored the sounds and opened the door.

Claudia O'Neill stood there. She smiled uncertainly. "We just put the paper to bed," she said. "It's on the press. I came to tell you, I am printing your editorial—on the front page— just about as you said it to me."

"I hope you're not asking for trouble."

She smiled wanly. "I guess we can't be safe all the time, can we?" Her lovely face was flushed, her eyes unable to meet his. She waited for him to ask her in.

He said, "I'm afraid you've chosen the wrong side, ma'am. You'll be better off if you stay away from me."

Claudia bit at her lip. She sighed and said, "Well, I just came to tell you, I've decided to help you, Mr. Long. As long as I can. As long as they'll let me."

Chapter 14

Longarm crept as close as possible to the clearing around the Gila River Cattle Company's north line camp. He crouched in the pine copse, staring down at the slab-sided shack, the lean-to, the corral and outhouse. It was not a place of many conveniences; it looked like exactly what it was, a place for line riders to sack out in.

Finding a record of the Gila River Cattle Company had been easy; it had not been as easy to ascertain that Gila River Cattle was owned by Don Hernán Salazar. But finally, he'd found that proof.

A couple of cow horses dozed in the pole corral. Smoke rose from the tin stovepipe jutting from the tarpaper roofing of the line shack. Otherwise, nothing stirred.

Longarm chewed on an unlit cheroot, watching the cabin in the clearing. In the mountains above, thunderheads boiled black and fat. Distantly, lightning crackled like firecrackers, soundless. The storm looked as if it were rolling toward him.

The wind increased, whistling in the pines and whipping dust in the clearing. Finally the door of the line shack opened and a tall, wide-shouldered black man with a thick chest and a potbelly came out. He wore only Levi's and longjohns, the shirt looking dingy and sweated.

The Negro went to the outhouse. Longarm used this moment to catfoot across the clearing and place himself against the blind side of the shack where he could watch the yard and corral.

At last, the black man emerged from the outhouse, buttoning his fly and yawning. Distant lightning flashed and he glanced toward it, wiping the back of his hand across his mouth.

Longarm let him get all the way to the door of the shack. Then he stepped around the corner of the hut and pressed his gun in the Negro's back.

The black tried to heel around, but Longarm thrust the gun harder. He said, "Just stand easy, George. I'm U.S. Marshal Custis Long."

"What you want with me?"

"You're the man who scalped and mutilated the McLoomis family, George."

A shudder went through the thick body, but the black man shook his head. "You crazy, Long? Indians massacred the Judge and his family. I heard about it. I went up there."

"You went back up there, George."

"You're talking crazy, man."

"No. Your three partners are in jail in Silver City, George, and they all say you did it. They said you bought a knife at Cohen's department store."

George was silent a long time. At last he swore. "I bought the knife, all right. But I didn't slice nobody. Lee Hill mutilated 'em—so it'd look like Apaches did it."

"Apaches don't ride shod horses, George. You hombres weren't real smart. We found where you waited, where you tied up. We got your buddies and they told us where to find you."

"Where's the rest of the posse?"

"There is no rest of the posse, George. I came up here for you by myself."

"You're lying. Lee and them boys ain't been caught. You're trying to trick me."

Longarm snapped handcuffs on Jefferson's thick wrists, securing his hands at the small of his back. "You better be smarter than that, George. We figured you'd like to tell me about it on the way back."

"Yeah? Why should I do that?"

"To save your neck, George. Somebody's going to hang for these murders. Lee and the boys turned against you, but if you're willing to tell me who did the killing—and how—I might be able to make it easy on you."

"You mean if I talk to you—I don't hang?"

"I'll see what I can do, George."

George began to talk on the way into Silver City. Rain began to fall harder and harder, but Longarm's spirits were high; he had his confession, which implicated three other Gila River Cattle Company cowboys. George didn't know who had set up the deal. Somebody had hired Lee Hill and promised to pay them all through Lee.

The rain was battering them furiously by the time they entered the town limits from the west. Loose clouds sailed, driven on the wind, like dead leaves littered across the gray sky.

As heavy as the rain was, Longarm could see that the real storm was still north of them, in the mountain ranges. Storm clouds, like brooding, ill-born monsters, slunk threateningly, black and misshapen, above the jagged horizon of the Mogollons.

The clouds raced faster and the rain pelted them. Longarm tied their horses at the hitch rail outside the County Building and prodded George ahead of him into the sheriff's office.

Deputy Len Hazelton's face went gray at the sight of Longarm. He began to shake his head. "Tyne come to me with a telegram," Hazelton said. "Telegram said the real Dan Watson had been captured two months ago in Laredo, Texas. Wasn't nothing I could do but let Wheeler go."

"You'll get your chance to defend yourself," Longarm said in a cold, dead tone. "In court."

The door to the sheriff's inner office opened and Henry Whitehill came out of it. He stared at George Jefferson, who stood with hands cuffed behind his back, rain dripping from sodden clothes and from the floppy brim of his hat. "I'm sorry about Watson, Long. What you got here?"

"This is George Jefferson. Bad-conduct discharge from the Ninth Cavalry. Works for Gila River Cattle. Along with Lee Hill, Frank Danzer, and King Roy, he attacked and killed Judge McLoomis and his family yesterday on the stage road to Lordsburg. I told Jefferson you had Hill, Danzer, and Roy in jail and they had confessed. George wants to turn state's evidence against his pals, as soon as your people round them up."

"I'll put Deputy Dan Turner on it," Whitehill said. "Right now."

Jefferson stared at Longarm. "You son of a bitch," he said. "You lied to me."

"That's the way it is, George," Longarm said. "When you start killing people, you can't trust anybody."

As Longarm was leaving the sheriff's office after George Jefferson had been booked and jailed, Sheriff Whitehill stopped him at the corridor door. "I saw your 'editorial' in the *Enterprise* this morning. Didn't like it much. But I didn't take as dim a view as some folks. I can tell you, vandals have destroyed the Enterprise office and printing plant. You never saw such a mess in your life as they made."

"How's Claudia O'Neill?"

"She's beaten pretty bad. They have her in Ladies' Hospital, over on Hudson Street. Al Huckworth is in the hospital too. Afraid they ruptured ol' Al's spleen. You can't call honest people in this town crooks, Mr. Long, and get away with it."

"All you people have done is proved that everything I've said about you is true," Longarm said. He turned and started from the office.

"Just a minute, Mr. Long." As Longarm put his hand on the doorknob, Whitehill's voice stopped him. Longarm looked over his shoulder.

"Yeah?"

"Whether you're right or not, Mr. Long, I ain't as hard set

166

against you as most—though I can see how you might cost me this election, and I'm damned if I can see how that's going to benefit Grant County. But I can tell you this. The whole town is against you now. Your life is in danger, from the minute you walk out of this office."

Longarm stared at the sheriff. After a moment, Whitehill's gaze drooped slightly. Longarm laughed coldly. "I reckon one way of dying is like another, Sheriff. A man could catch fatal pneumonia in this rain."

"With you, it's most apt to be lead poisoning, Long."

"See you in hell, Sheriff."

Longarm rode, head down, in the middle of the street. When he came to Main, he had to dismount and lead his horse to higher ground east of the thoroughfare.

He paused for a moment, looking back. Small trees, uprooted and washed out from the broken places above Main, were being swept along in the driving current.

Lightning crashed, white and bleak, followed by deafening peals of thunder that shook the earth.

Far up Main Street, he could see the gound begin to crumble under the walks, falling in great hunks into the torrent. Leading his horse, he went along Broadway to Hudson, and then along Hudson to Ladies' Hospital. Water stood a foot or so deep in Hudson Street, but the avenue wasn't being eroded away as Main was.

Claudia O'Neill lay battered and bruised in a private hospital room when Longarm walked in.

She turned her face away. "Don't look at me," she said. "I look like a monster."

"Not to me," Longarm told her. "You want to know what you look like to me?"

"What?"

"Like a pretty lady, like a truly beautiful woman, who did her job and got savaged for it."

"I was right, wasn't I?"

"That won't help heal your face."

"No. But poor old Al Huckworth, they nearly killed him. I guess they just meant to 'warn' me. Well, we tried, Mr.

Long. We just can't stop them. They're too rich, too big, too conscienceless."

He smiled and held her hand. "You and me," he said. "We're still here. They've got consciences, whether they know it or not. And we're not through yet."

"I'm afraid I am. They wrecked the plant. It would take Al a month to straighten out the type trays alone. And I don't know if the presses can be repaired."

"I'll go over and look at the plant," he promised. "You've got advertisers. They'll help you get back in business."

"Why should they?"

"Because they know this kind of thing could happen to them. Or if they don't know it yet, they'll know it before I'm through talking to them."

Her hand tightened on his. "Take care of yourself. I've heard terrible things . . . they are out to kill you."

"I've got you—and the rain—on my side," Longarm said. "I'll keep moving. They've got to come find me, and when they do, I figure the odds will even out a little."

"God help you," she said. She bit her lip. "If you do go to my plant, would you do something for me?"

"Sure."

"My files. My old newspapers. I need them terribly if I am to—to stay in business. Even if I only print the kind of newspaper they want—with recipes for rhubarb pie." She sniffled and shook her head. "Could you see how many of the file papers you can save? Maybe put them in boxes, and up on shelves?"

The storm spread, the thunder crackling and reverberating off the hills, the lightning turning the world a dazzling white.

When Longarm crossed Main on Yankie Street, headed east toward Texas Street and the *Enterprise* office, he found Main looking like a wide creek at full crest.

A six-foot break in the sump of Main Street was like a bottomless crevice. Longarm had to swim across, leading his horse. He returned the animal to the Elephant Corral, which was a livery stable, and walked over to the *Enterprise* building.

The front door stood ajar, hanging like a broken wing.

Longarm closed it against the wind and rain, and went about lighting lamps and lanterns against the dark and chill.

At first he stood round-shouldered, gazing hopelessly about, doubting that anything in the place could be saved. But the longer he studied the vandalism, the more hopeful he became. The vandals had jerked the type drawers from their racks and spilled type everywhere, but the type was in good shape, and the drawers usable. Time. Time and painstaking work would heal most of the wounds in the typesetting area.

The hooligans had smashed the presses with axes, but the machines were dented more than destroyed. Plates and rollers would have to be replaced, but most of the presses looked as if they could be repaired.

In the front office, the intruders had overturned Claudia's rolltop desk and yanked down the wooden shelves. Stacks of newspapers littered the floor, but they hadn't ripped any of them up.

Longarm lifted the rolltop desk and set it against the wall. He replaced blotter, inkstand, pens, and pencil holders.

He stood the wooden shelves up against the walls again, and began to stack the newspapers on them. Putting them in order would have to wait for another day, but at least the files would be off the floor.

Headlines from the past snagged at his attention, caught his interest, but he set the papers aside. He couldn't stop to read. He found the paper that Claudia had shown him the first time he was in this office, headlining the death of her husband. She'd been a pretty brave little lady then. She had written that the mining interests had warned Ephraim that he would be "removed" if he printed certain material that the mining people called "libelous." There was even a short article in which she quoted W. W. Meriman as vowing that neither he nor any miner he knew would stoop to murder to remove opposition.

Longarm shivered, remembering the way Meriman had sworn he would buy loyalty, but would never buy killers to remove his opposition. Meriman made a convincing statement of his position. But in the face of all that had happened, it left you wondering what in hell you could believe in this town, Longarm thought.

He placed the newspaper on a stack on the high shelf. Another headline clutched at his attention:.

WILFRED PYLES DIES

Wealthy Ex-Telegrapher Under Indictment

According to the obituary, written by Ephraim O'Neill, Wilfred Pyles had died wealthy. Pyles owned much of Main Street, as well as stocks, bonds, and interests in certain mines and smelters. He had been under indictment at the time of his death—from heart failure, according to the county coroner—for having misused his position with Western Union to enrich himself. They had proved that Pyles had kept separate copies of most of the confidential telegrams that went through his office.

Longarm stood there a long time, gripping the newspaper and staring at it. It was as if old self-righteous, holier-than-thou Ephraim O'Neill were trying to tell him something from the grave.

The broken front door scraped the cement flooring as it was pushed stealthfully open. Drawing his gun, Longarm sank quickly to his knees.

The pistol showed first in the doorway. Then a man's form. A voice roared, "Hold it, thief! I caught you!"

Whoever it was, the gunman telegraphed his move. The barrel of the firearm tilted and Longarm sprawled forward, hitting the floor as the man fired six times without hesitating.

Chapter 15

The fusillade of bullets whizzed over Longarm's head. He shoved his face into the damp planks of the flooring. The gunfire was louder than the thunder, closer than the blindingly white flashes of lightning, and thudded around him like hailstones.

When he counted off the sixth shot, Longarm shifted his position on the floor. Before his assailant could withdraw his gun from the doorway, and before the echoes of the barrage had died away, Longarm raised his Colt, took aim at the darkness beyond that bucking gun, and fired.

The gunman gasped, dropped the gun, and then fell forward into the printing office. He lay sodden and dripping on the floor, his hat at an angle off his balding head.

Longarm waited only long enough to be certain the man was alone. Staying low, he inched across the office to where the man lay. He recognized the gunman as one of Tuttle's town deputies; he didn't know his name. He put his hand on the man's chest. There was no heartbeat.

He wasted no more time; he had done all he could do here; he had to get out of this lighted place if he was to stay alive. Bent over below window level, he went about the office, blowing out the lamps and lanterns.

When the office was dark again, he returned to the broken front door. He dragged the dead deputy outside the door and left him there in the darkness, then he closed the door and secured it as well as he could.

A blinding blaze of lightning illumined the world, and Longarm pressed himself against the wall. Then, pulling his hat low over his eyes and setting himself against the torrential downpour of rain and hail, he ran along the darkened Yankie Street toward Main.

Despite the ferocity of the storm, the town was alive with people, and by the time he reached the corner of Main Street, he saw why. The street was caving in and washing away in the raging torrent.

He stood, awed, staring at the torn earth eight or nine blocks north of him, where a huge gorge was being chewed out of the land at a place where, even in the darkness, it seemed that two tumultuous rivers joined, ripping out everything before them. Live oak trees trembled, then plunged into the boiling cauldron of the floodwaters.

Up at the top of the street, one could see where a couple of houses had already been sucked into the river and bounced along on the current until they struck submerged obstacles. They hung there until the swirling water ate away the barriers, and then they toppled forward again.

People were wailing as if they were witnessing the very end of the world.

Many people with horses and wagons were trying to save what they could from buildings in the path of the frenzied waters, but not yet inundated.

Awed, Longarm watched the walks yanked up and tossed like petals on the headlong current. Once the walks were gone, the earth was chewed away from the supports of buildings and they first sagged forward, then slipped and finally tumbled into the cataract.

People ran, yelling mindlessly, in the exploding darkness. They were helpless against the fury of the water. Most of them had seen flash floods, but none had ever encountered flooding with the violence and force of this raging river. It was as if all the waters from all the hills and mountains above them had fed into the two furious streams that converged at the head of Main Street, ripping, tearing, eroding.

Longarm glanced around, unsure what to do. There was no chance of moving on Main Street. Those who had tried to cross it in the past hour had lost their lives, and the gorge widened as more and more trees, walks, and buildings crumbled into its irresistible turbulence.

He saw that his only chance of getting as far north as Market Street and the Exchange Hotel was through the alley behind the buildings.

As he turned around, somebody yelled his name from the darkness. "Longarm! Look out behind you!"

The warning yell, a peal of thunder, a white flash of lightning, and the blaze of gunfire from the alley behind him all occurred in the same instant.

Longarm flung himself against the wall of the building next to him, and slid down it. The gunman fired again.

Longarm held his breath and fired into the middle of that blossoming muzzle flash.

Suddenly, from the darkness of the alley, J. Z. Banning leaped up. He ran strangely, crouched over, one arm pressed against his belly.

Banning held his gun out before him, firing wildly toward Longarm. Longarm returned the fire. His bullet struck Banning in the thigh, collapsing his leg under him. He fell to one knee, and then forced himself up again.

By now he was beyond Longarm, at the corner of Main Street, bracing himself against a wall.

The gunman was screaming at the top of his lungs. He fired his gun toward Longarm until it was empty, then threw it to the street.

Banning drew his second gun and tried to lift it. Longarm fired. His bullet struck the adobe wall within inches of Banning's head.

Banning, yelling in terror, leaped away from the bullet,

173

firing mindlessly. Longarm fired again and Banning lunged away. This time he went sprawling into the swift-running torrent. He was there for only the space of a breath, screaming and waving his arms. And then he was gone.

Crouched low in the shadows, Longarm reloaded his Colt, searching the darkness for whoever had yelled the warning. "We're quits, Longarm," Les Shaw shouted from the darkness. "They're after you. They're all after you. They mean to get you this time."

Longarm didn't bother to answer. Men were running toward him in the ankle-deep water of Yankie Street. He ran toward the alleyway, and threw himself into it as a barrage of gunfire exploded around him.

The gunmen were running in the street and firing toward the alley. He found one of them crossing Yankie toward him. A white blaze of lightning illuminated the man and Longarm shot him.

He did not stay long enough for any of the gunmen to fire at the flash of his gun in the dark. Staying close against the wall, he ran north through knee-deep water. It was like trying to run in high surf.

Holding his gun, he pressed himself into a recess in a wall, watching both ways. At Yankie, he saw three men cautiously entering the alley and running toward him, staying close to the dark walls as he had.

As he moved to run toward Market Street, two men with guns came into the alley from that direction. He slumped back into the shadows.

One of the men at the south end of the alley fired and the men leaped for cover, cursing and yelling. "Don't shoot, you damn fools! It's us!" one of them called.

A flash of lightning clearly lit one of the men at the north end of the alley. Longarm fired at the man and heard his body splash heavily in the foot-deep water of the alley.

A second man lunged out of the shadows and raced back toward Market Street. Longarm steadied his gun and squeezed the trigger, and the man sprawled forward beyond the end of the alley and lay still.

The three men south of him hesitated as they saw their two mates taken out of action.

Longarm drew a deep breath and held it. He had to get out of here, or they would close in on him from both ends of the alley. Still holding his breath, he slid around the edge of the wall and ran north toward Market Street.

As he came out of the alley onto Market Street, lightning flared white, and guns roared from the alley behind him, from the windows of the Exchange hotel, and from the passage behind it. A withering barrage of gunfire crackled along the street.

Longarm spun against the building and then rolled along it toward the turbulent cataract at Main, watching for movement, any target in the night around him. A curtain moved in an upstairs window of the hotel, and he flicked a shot toward it, running east as he fired.

Guns rattled again from the darkness behind him. For one eternal moment, he stood illumined in a white-flaring burst of lightning. The guns blasted again.

Longarm went racing toward Main Street. At the crumbling walkway, he hurtled outward into the torrent.

He struck the water and was thrust along as wildly as a leaf in a storm. He fought helplessly against the force of water.

A log was swept down upon him on the ferocious current. He clutched at it, snagged it, and pulled himself against it. By now he had been carried almost a block on the foaming river.

Clinging to the log, he was hurled along on the surface. The water level was up almost to the windows of every building along the street, and rising.

The log, like an awkward ark, sailed into what had been the porch overhang of a building. The front door stood open, and water rushed into it higher than the windowsills.

Longarm bumped against a porch upright. He released the log and it bobbed away on the rising current. Everything around him was blackness. He clung to the support, feeling the building trembling as water undermined it and ate away the earth from its underpinnings.

He put his feet against the upright and hurled himself toward the open door and the comparatively calm waters beyond. The raging tide yanked at him, but he fought, grabbing the doorjamb and pulling himself through it.

For the first time he realized he was in the Western Union

office; the place was deserted and rapidly filling with water. He waded, sloshing and fighting his way to the rear door, and went out of it into the swift current of foot-deep water in the alley.

Girls, carrying what belongings they could in their arms, ran out of the rear door of the Fandango Saloon and crowded into a waiting coach that blocked the alley, both of its doors standing open.

Rain struck with blistering force, rattling on rooftops, pounding on the coach, and peppering the black, swift-running water. All along the alleyway, people screamed, called, or wailed in terror. Whole blocks of buildings above Kelly Street had disappeared into the black, overflowing pit, and its sides were still caving in, great chunks of land being chewed away by the savage waters. The Fandango Saloon already tilted at a slight angle.

He pushed past the girls fighting their way out of the rear door of the saloon. He had no clear idea what he wanted here. He felt as if he were propelled by a will he didn't understand and could not control.

He found Nellie Pyles in the big barroom of her fancy house. She stood on the tilting floor, her hand on the polished bar.

He said, "Hello, Nellie."

She stared at him as if she had never seen him before. "My beautiful place," she said. "It's going to be carried away."

"Looks like it," he agreed. "Everything along the street's gone."

"But this is mine," she said in an odd, empty voice.

"You double-crossed me, Nellie," he said.

"What?" She looked up, forcing her gaze to focus on him.

"It doesn't matter now. Everybody tried to beat me, but you pretended to be my friend. And all the time you were reading the telegraph key. You knew what was going on. You got word to the right people. For the right price, Nellie?"

She shrugged, drumming her fingers on the bar. "A girl needs money," was all she said.

"All that drumming of your fingers wasn't nerves, was it, Nellie? You had no nerves. You'd learned telegraphy from your husband. You could read it as fast as it came in next door."

She gazed at him, almost pityingly. "They didn't want you here, Longarm. They wanted to know what you sent out, and what came in to you. They were willing to pay. What was a girl to do?"

He shrugged. "That's how you knew I was on Meriman's stage, huh? And old Chisum must have wired that he was bringing ten thousand dollars. Was that a little side deal between you and Les Shaw? Shaw would collect for stealing my identification, and the two of you would split the ten grand?"

"That's right, Long." Les Shaw's voice came from behind him, at the door to the rear of the saloon.

Longarm turned, staring at Les. Shaw stood, looking like a drowned rat, his gun extended in his left hand and supported by his crippled right arm. The gun was fixed on Longarm.

"They're coming for you, Long," Les Shaw said. "It don't matter now, but they're coming. They have to go around the break at the top of Main, but they're coming. But I got here first. They've doubled the reward for you, Long. Sorry, but Nellie and me need the money."

At the instant that Les tilted his gun, the huge building shifted violently forward. Nellie screamed, grabbing at the bar. Longarm fell against it, firing his Colt.

Les fired, but his bullet went into the floor. The hostler sprawling, sliding across the floor toward the low front wall, along with tables, chairs, and everything else that wasn't nailed down.

The building shifted again. Longarm scrambled at the long upward angle, going through the rear door. As he stepped to the ground, the building tilted behind him again and, with a screaming of tortured timber, lurched into the flood. The roiling waters surged immediately into the cavity it left behind, and the building collapsed and disintegrated as though it were made of matchsticks.

Chapter 16

The rain had slacked off slightly by daybreak, but the Silver City flats were still inundated.

Longarm awoke from a restless doze, his head on Tuttle's old desk in the marshal's office on Hudson Street. Behind him, locked in cells, lounged Dan Watson and another of the hired-gun deputies. They had been in the office last night when Longarm decided he'd be safest and driest in the place where his would-be killers would least likely expect to find him.

On the poorly protected stoop outside the marshal's office, he had drawn his gun, slowly turned the knob, and thrust the door open wide.

Like some apparition from hell, he stepped into the doorway, his gun fixed on the two deputies inside. One of them was Dan Watson. They made no effort to oppose him. One deputy was slouched with his head back, his feet up on his desk. Dan was pouring himself a cup of coffee.

They turned and stared at Longarm, offering no resistance.

He disarmed them and locked them in cells in the cellblock. He returned to the front office, barred the front door, loaded all the guns he could find, and set himself for any siege.

It did not come. Periodically he heard the thunderous capsizing of buildings over on Main Street.

In the dark hours before dawn, as his clothes began to dry in the pleasant warmth of the stove fire, he sagged, his head on his arms, and slept at Tuttle's desk.

"They'll get you!" Watson yelled from the rear cell. "You ain't getting out of here alive!"

Longarm yawned. He walked over to the bars dividing the office from the cellblock. "You best shut up and start praying, Watson."

"Yeah, Long? What for?"

"That they don't try to break in here. First one tries to break down that front door, I'm shooting you."

There was a taut, brief silence. Then Watson yelled, "You son of a bitch!"

"That's the way it is in this business, Watson," Longarm said. "You can't even trust the lawmen anymore."

He heard the sounds of horses and men out in Hudson Street. Holding his gun at his side, Longarm strode to the barred front window and peered out.

A company of soldiers from Fort Bayard, armed and mounted, stood at parade rest in the street outside the marshal's office.

At the head of the column, Longarm recognized the arrow-straight form of the young lieutenant, Black Jack Pershing.

Relief flooding through him, Longarm crossed the room, threw the bolts and thrust open the door.

Grinning, he walked out onto the stoop.

The rain pelted down, but the sun shone through the downpour.

"My God, Pershing," Longarm said, "I'm glad to see you."

"You taken over the town marshal's office?" Pershing asked. He swung down from the saddle, looped his reins over the hitch rail, and came up the steps, dripping.

Longarm shrugged. "Thought I might as well."

Pershing removed his hat as they walked into the office. He

180

slapped it against his thigh and stood looking around. "Figured I might use this as my headquarters while we're stationed in Silver City."

"Stationed here? You mean General Hatch changed his mind?"

Pershing grinned. "General Hatch never got where he is by changing his mind, Long. No, my company is detailed here to guard against looting. Our orders from General Hatch and Governor Wallace are clear. We are to shoot any looters. But I figured you'd see this as good news."

"Getting what we wanted—under a different name." Longarm smiled and nodded.

"That's right. My troops and I are here to guard against looting, but I figure our presence will quiet the whole town down, and guarantee the quiet kind of election that you see as essential."

Longarm nodded. "I guarantee it."

Pershing looked around, smiling. "I figured that would please you, Long."

Longarm laughed. "I say it again, Pershing, you'll go far in this man's army—if they don't court-martial you."

"If they don't court-martial me," Pershing agreed.

Pershing ordered his men to dismount. He opened the cell-block doors and used the corridor and all the cells, except the one where Watson and the other deputy marshal were incarcerated, as quarters for his men.

He detailed squads for all the streets that crossed where Main Street once had been.

He sat at the big rolltop desk, and shoved his hand into his inner pocket. "Oh, by the way, Long. When the telegraph went out here in Silver City yesterday, all traffic was rerouted through our telegraph service at Fort Bayard. I've got some telegrams here for you."

Longarm took them and thanked the young lieutenant. He propped himself against one of the desks that had been appropriated by a second lieutenant and several noncommissioned officers.

The first telegram was from Lew Wallace, and expressed the governor's regrets that he was powerless to demand army assistance in the Silver City area; Wallace explained that he

181

could override General Hatch only in case of a national emergency, such as an enemy attack by a foreign nation.

The second telegram was from Billy Vail, and was typically terse:

'U S ATTORNEY AT SANTA FE AGREES TO ACT ON SPANISH LAND GRANT VIOLATIONS IN GRANT COUNTY STOP PROCEED TO SANTA FE AND MAKE FULL REPORT TO U S ATTY THEN REPORT TO DENVER OFFICE IMMEDIATELY REPEAT IMMEDIATELY STOP WELL DONE STOP VAIL U S MARSHAL DENV"

Longarm and Pershing walked into the Ladies' Hospital, next door to the jail. Victims of the flood were lying on cots, stretchers, and piles of blankets and donated clothing, while others were sitting or standing about, staring vacantly.

Longarm's inquiries eventually yielded the information that Claudia O'Neill had been released and had returned to her home at the rear of the *Enterprise* offices on Yankie Street.

Longarm and Pershing rode along Kelly Street to the brink of the big ditch that once had been Main Street. The torrent was swirling less furiously, but it still chewed at the broken edges of land, and it had swallowed every building the length of the avenue.

Longarm and the young officer dismounted. Holding the reins of their horses, they stood with the silent, gaping people, staring at what had, one day earlier, been the busiest thoroughfare in the busy town.

"Good Lord," Pershing said in a low, reverent voice.

Longarm nodded. He found this same hushed sense of awe in the people around him. He remained watchful, but it was as if the fight had been washed out of even the roughest of the citizenry.

They gazed in awed silence at the swirling waters in the vast gorge. Every vestige of the street had been washed away. The canyon gouged out by the floodwaters was a mile in length. In places it stretched more than one hundred feet wide, and when the waters receded, the arroyo would remain, fifty feet deep.

All the businesses and homes along both sides of Main Street had been washed into the mile-long cauldron. The dance-hall where the first law court had convened, the first church, and the first school were gone, as were stores, saloons, hotels and banks.

Longarm shook hands with the young lieutenant. "I'll leave you here, Black Jack. Thanks, and good luck to you."

"You going to be all right?"

Longarm sighed and nodded. "Yes. Looks like this flood has taken all the fight out of these people for the moment. I'll say goodbye to a friend of mine and catch the morning train out. I'm kind of anxious to get to Santa Fe. A lot of changes got to be made around here, and we might as well get them started."

Longarm was shocked to find Claudia, her face battered and her left arm in a sling, sitting at her desk in the shambles of her office. He was even more astonished to see Al Huckworth, bent over like an old man, but working with three temporary typesetters and printers.

Claudia looked up and smiled. "Thanks for taking care of everything here, Longarm."

"Shouldn't you be in bed?"

"That's the best offer I've had since Ephraim died, Mr. Long," Claudia said.

He laughed. "You were pretty battered."

"It doesn't matter. Al and I have to get out an extra edition."

"I know you're busy," Longarm said. "I won't keep you. I reckon I was hoping to find you still in bed."

She looked up and smiled at him, her eyes gentle in her bruised face. "You missed your chance, Mr. Long, when I came to your hotel room that night."

"I didn't like to take advantage of a widow."

"That was the reason I was there, you know. I got to thinking about you...I couldn't stay away...I had so little...with Ephraim...I felt as if I didn't know anything at all. I could think only that...that you would teach me...and I had so much to learn." She sighed, smiled and looked up at him. "Maybe you'll come back this way someday, Longarm."

"I hope so, with all my heart," he said.

She sighed again. "Well, if you don't, we all have something in our lives to regret, don't we?"

Look for

LONGARM ON THE BARBARY COAST

forty-first novel in the bold
LONGARM series from Jove

LONGARM

Explore the exciting Old West with
one of the men who made it wild!

_____ 06576-5	LONGARM #1	$2.25
_____ 06807-1	LONGARM ON THE BORDER #2	$2.25
_____ 06809-8	LONGARM AND THE WENDIGO #4	$2.25
_____ 06810-1	LONGARM IN THE INDIAN NATION #5	$2.25
_____ 06950-7	LONGARM IN LINCOLN COUNTY #12	$2.25
_____ 06070-4	LONGARM IN LEADVILLE #14	$1.95
_____ 06155-7	LONGARM ON THE YELLOWSTONE #18	$1.95
_____ 06951-5	LONGARM IN THE FOUR CORNERS #19	$2.25
_____ 06627-3	LONGARM AT ROBBER'S ROOST #20	$2.25
_____ 06628-1	LONGARM AND THE SHEEPHERDERS #21	$2.25
_____ 07141-2	LONGARM AND THE GHOST DANCERS #22	$2.25
_____ 07142-0	LONGARM AND THE TOWN TAMER #23	$2.25
_____ 07363-6	LONGARM AND THE RAILROADERS #24	$2.25
_____ 07066-1	LONGARM ON THE MISSION TRAIL #25	$2.25
_____ 06952-3	LONGARM AND THE DRAGON HUNTERS #26	$2.25
_____ 07265-6	LONGARM AND THE RURALES #27	$2.25
_____ 06629-X	LONGARM ON THE HUMBOLDT #28	$2.25

Available at your local bookstore or return this form to:

JOVE
Book Mailing Service
P.O. Box 690, Rockville Centre, NY 11571

Please send me the titles checked above. I enclose _____
Include $1.00 for postage and handling if one book is ordered; 50¢ per book for
two or more. California, Illinois, New York and Tennessee residents please add
sales tax.

NAME _____

ADDRESS _____

CITY _____ STATE/ZIP _____

(allow six weeks for delivery) 5

LONGARM

Explore the exciting Old West with one of the men who made it wild!